"From this point on, expect the unexpected. That's how you'll stay alive."

His bluntness made a chill run up her spine. Agent Goodluck stood straight, shoulders thrown back—a warrior's stance. The black leather jacket enhanced his powerful build. Everything about him spoke of unwavering self-assurance.

The full impact of what had happened slammed into her again. Men she'd never seen before had tried to kill her. One of the gunmen had actually died less than ten feet from her. What was worse, she might still be a target.

Tremors ripped through her and she folded her arms around her middle, as if trying to hug herself.

A heartbeat later, Kyle threw his black leather jacket over her shoulders.

"No, I'm okay," she managed.

"You're holding it together, but that's not the same as okay," he said, his voice gentle.

Maybe not, but she couldn't show him how badly she wanted him to wrap his powerful arms around her and never let go.

UNDERCOVER WARRIOR

Aimée Thurlo

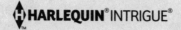
HARLEQUIN® INTRIGUE®

Every author has special friends. This is our way of thanking those of you who have made our work possible through a smile, an encouraging word or by simply believing in us.

With that in mind, this book is dedicated to DZ, Sheila and Duffy.

Recycling programs for this product may not exist in your area.

ISBN-13: 978-0-373-74826-6

UNDERCOVER WARRIOR

Copyright © 2014 by Aimée and David Thurlo

Printed in U.S.A.

ABOUT THE AUTHOR

Aimée Thurlo is an internationally known bestselling author of mystery and romantic suspense novels. She's the winner of a Career Achievement Award from *RT Book Reviews,* a New Mexico Book Award in contemporary fiction and a Willa Cather Award in the same category.

Aimée was born in Havana, Cuba, and lives with her husband of forty-three years in Corrales, New Mexico, in a rural neighborhood filled with horses, alpacas, camels and other assorted livestock. Her husband, David, was raised on the Navajo Indian Nation. His background and cultural knowledge inspire many of her stories.

Books by Aimée Thurlo

CAST OF CHARACTERS

Kyle Goodluck—His last assignment for NCIS ended in tragedy. Now he was at home, working undercover, on the trail of terrorists. His chief suspect was dead, and the only witness, Erin Barrett, was under his protection. Erin was temptation itself, dangerous to be around—no matter where her loyalties lay.

Erin Barrett—Her boss, Hank Leland, was killed right before her eyes, but she'd been rescued just in time by the rugged Navajo man who insisted he was with the IRS. All she wanted in life was to raise enough money to buy her own farm. Now her life was a nightmare, and her only hope rested with a man she couldn't trust. Kyle was destined to break her heart...if they lived long enough.

Preston Bowman—He was a Hartley detective, and Kyle was his foster brother. Together they had to learn why Hank Leland had been killed, and what his connection was to a terrorist cell planning an imminent attack. Who were Hank's contacts, and why were they so interested in Erin Barrett?

Bruce Leland—Even Hank, his brother, couldn't trust him, and after Hank was killed, Bruce was caught breaking into his home. Bruce was clearly a man with a gambling addiction, but was he also a traitor?

Frieda Martinez—Hank's flashy girlfriend easily attracted men, first Bruce, then his brother. Yet the moment he was killed she dropped out of sight. Now the search was on for the woman who held the key to murder...and maybe more.

Ed Huff—He was the bartender at the Quarter Horse Bar where Frieda worked as a waitress. He knew she was trouble from the start. The woman had secrets, but Ed knew how to use those to his own advantage. Just how far he could push her was anyone's guess.

Joe Pacheco—Joe was a retired police officer well known in the community. Now he worked for Secure Construction, Hank's company. When Hank was killed, Joe became a target. He needed help, but Joe didn't trust the Feds, NCIS included.

Ron Mora—The paralegal worked for Moe Jenner, Hank's attorney. When the well-known lawyer disappeared, Ron refused to help them find his boss. Either Ron was covering for Jenner, or something illegal was going on.

Chapter One

Kyle Goodluck liked living on the edge. He carried his NCIS badge with honor, stood tall and faced things squarely. He'd served his country well, first as a marine and now as a federal agent. This time the case he was working on had brought him back home.

Kyle watched his brother, Hartley Police Detective Preston Bowman, take a call. Preston's face was characteristically impassive and hard. Once finished, he put the cell phone back in his pocket.

"Sorry for the interruption," Preston said. "Now talk to me. What's going on? I thought you were going to turn in your badge and come home for good this time."

He wouldn't lie to his brother, but Kyle wasn't above sidestepping the issue. "You know how it goes. Sometimes you have to step back and think hard about long-term decisions, particularly ones that'll affect your future."

"So you're not ready to talk about what's really going on."

He laughed. "Nothing much gets past you, does it? Forgot who I was dealing with for a sec."

"You and I have always been able to read each other," Preston said. "I'm guessing you're under orders, but this is *my* turf. You may need my help and HPD's cooperation somewhere along the way. Keeping us in the dark is a bad idea."

"I hear you—loud and clear." Preston's warning was unmistakable. He wouldn't take it well if an undercover op went down under his nose and he knew nothing about it. Unfortunately, orders were orders.

"I better be shoving off," Preston said. "Where are you planning to stay? You can use the ranch house at Copper Canyon, if you want. We've continued with the upgrades and it's in pretty decent shape right now. You've also got Hosteen Silver's letter waiting for you there…," he said, pausing for a reaction.

"No way I'm opening that, buddy. The first four of us who did ended up getting married. I'm leaving that envelope unopened in the desk drawer for the foreseeable future."

"Coward."

"Guilty," Kyle answered laughing. "Hosteen Silver was a good *hataalii*," he said, using the Navajo word for medicine man. "He could do some amazing things, like predicting future events, but some-times it's better not to know."

"There's a lot to be said for advance notice," Preston said. "Forewarned is forearmed."

"Maybe, but my work, my life, is all based on what happens minute by minute. The future…well, it's still going to be there waiting for me to arrive."

"I hear you," Preston answered.

Kyle phone's rang, and seeing the display, he glanced back at his brother. "I've got to take this."

Preston stood. "I'm going to work. You know how to get hold of me if you need me."

As Preston left the table, Kyle answered the call. "Kyle here."

"We've had a new development," Martin Hamilton said. "Call me back on a secure phone."

The next thing he heard was a dial tone.

Slipping into his black leather jacket—the early-morning fall breeze was brisk—Kyle walked out to his service-provided SUV. He'd arrived about three hours ahead of the man he was supposed to tail, and had found the $100K prize waiting for him at the airport. His ride had come equipped with bulletproof windows, integral ceramic and Kevlar armor, a special mobile data terminal and satellite phone in the center console. GPS tracking gear was also hidden within the body, so his exact location would always be known to any agency with the right equipment.

Under the seat was an easy access M4 selective fire assault rifle with night vision capability and three thirty-round magazines. The spare-tire compartment contained tear gas, smoke and flash-bang grenades beside a first-aid and survival kit that would provide a week of food and water for two people. No spare tire was needed because they were all run-flat, immune to road hazards, spike belts and any weapons smaller than fifty caliber.

He picked up the satellite phone and entered the number. It was answered almost immediately at the other end by a female voice he recognized.

"Hello, Kyle," a rich, sultry voice greeted. "In place yet?"

"You bet. Just heard the boss wants to talk."

"I know. Don't I always? Patching you through now."

A moment later, a male voice came through clearly. "Regarding your target, Lieutenant Henry Leland. Any suspicious activity, any contacts?"

"No. This morning Leland's at Secure Construction. I've monitored his movements since his arrival. I'm currently down the street. He's there with his regular staff."

"Unless there's a specific reason for keeping him under surveillance, I suggest you break cover and meet up with him. He just called NCIS and asked for our help. He says he's being blackmailed by terrorists."

"Interesting development. What are my orders?"

"Check out his story, then stick to him like glue. Find out every detail of what's going on, and keep me in the loop. Leland just spent weeks in Spain at a U.S. naval base, working in restricted areas. We could be talking about a major breach in security."

"Copy that."

Kyle switched on the ignition, pulled out of the parking lot and drove down the street, alert for anything that might seem off or unusual. Nothing drew his attention. It was just another weekday morning in Hartley, New Mexico, a town just off the rez in the Four Corners region of the state.

This section of town was industrial, and most of the businesses were oil and gas field related. There were container-storage or building-supply warehouses and the occasional hole-in-the-wall fast-food place or gas station.

Kyle approached Secure Construction's five-acre, fenced compound from the east, passing the large warehouse and model structures, which were facing the street for maximum exposure. Ahead was the big double gate, parking lot and offices. All the buildings were constructed from the strong, corrugated metal-ceramic laminate components the company had built its reputation upon.

Making a right hand turn through the open gates into the parking lot, Kyle noted two vehicles in front of the office. One was Hank Leland's

Silverado pickup, the same truck Kyle had bugged, followed here from the airport last night and, lastly, to Leland's home. This morning its travel route had been more direct—home to office.

Just then a man in a light jacket and ball cap stepped out of the office's front entrance, Leland right behind him. Another man was on Leland's heels. Behind them, a woman was being forcibly pulled along by a third man.

Kyle recognized the stunning brunette from her file photo. It was Erin Barrett, Leland's office manager. Either Leland and the woman had just been arrested by undercover cops, or something was seriously wrong. His gut went with the latter option.

Kyle whipped his SUV around and skidded to a stop, placing his vehicle between him and the people coming down the sidewalk.

The man closest to him suddenly raised a pistol and pointed it at Kyle. "Stay in the car!" he ordered.

"Help!" the woman screamed.

Operating on instinct and training, Kyle threw open his door, reaching for his holstered Glock at the same time his feet touched the asphalt.

The men opened fire and he ducked down, moving forward behind the engine block as he heard bullets slapping against the passenger's side of his SUV. Taking a quick glance around the front end bumper, he saw Hank and the woman trying to pull free of their captors.

All three men had pistols out now, pointed in his direction. As Kyle ducked below the engine block, two more rounds whistled just over the hood. Kyle hit the ground, rolled left, and brought up his .40 caliber Glock.

The kidnappers sidestepped to their right, holding their hostages in front of them. They were moving too quickly for him to get a clear shot, so he rolled back to the right under the open door, jumped up and reached into the SUV. Holstering the Glock, he unhooked the latch holding the M4 assault rifle in place beneath the seat, and brought out the weapon.

Kyle ran around to the rear of his vehicle, still staying behind cover. He fed a round into the chamber, and thumbed off the safety, aiming his weapon as he came into view. The kidnappers had already slipped out of sight around the far corner of the office building, pulling along their hostages.

In a crouch, Kyle hurried to the opposite end of the building, veering to his right, sights on the back corner, waiting for someone to poke their head around.

He went down on one knee, and waited, finger on the trigger. Suddenly someone hurtled into view. His training forced him to ID the target before firing, and in that split second he saw it was the woman, Erin. She'd been shoved out to draw his fire.

"Hug the wall," he yelled to her, firing at the corner of the building just to the right of her. There was a groan and a man staggered out into the open, pistol falling from his outstretched hand as he clutched his chest.

It wasn't Hank—he'd known it wouldn't be. Only the bad guys would have pushed Erin out as a target.

Whirling around to his left, he heard then saw another of the armed men who'd circled back around the front of the building. As the man raised his pistol and fired, Kyle dodged, stepping toward the side of the building and out of his line of sight. The bullet tore off a chunk of building corner, but whistled behind him.

Kyle ran to the woman, who was crouched low, hugging the wall and staring in wide-eyed shock at the man on the ground in front of her. Kyle could tell at a glance that the gunman wouldn't be getting back up—at least not in this world. "Stay down. They're going to circle back around to the front!"

Just to be sure, Kyle took a quick glance around the back, and, as he'd guessed, nobody was there anymore. He stepped closer, placing himself between Erin and the front, his M4 in position to take out anyone stupid enough to look around the corner.

"They've got Hank!" she whispered, reaching for the pistol on the ground. She pulled back the slide just enough to verify a round was in the chamber, then checked the safety.

Surprised, he looked directly at her. "You know how to use that?"

"I was born and raised in rural New Mexico. Of course I do."

He gave her a quick grin. Beautiful and gutsy. He liked her already. "Okay. Watch yourself," he said, never taking his eyes off the corner as he stepped forward.

Crouching low, he inched around and aimed his weapon at the two men holding Hank between them. Both were looking away, one at the far corner, the other at the street.

Silently, he moved across the gravel and managed to outflank them, placing himself in a position to cut them off if they ran for the street exit. "Put down your weapons or I'll drop you!" he yelled.

Both spun around and fired, one shot shattering an office window behind him, the other tugging at Kyle's left shoulder, ripping fabric not flesh.

The sudden distraction gave Hank Leland a chance. He broke free and ran for his life toward the street.

Hearing screeching tires as a gray van raced into the parking lot, Kyle hit the ground and rolled. "Hank, watch out!" he yelled seconds too late.

The van's passenger-side front end suddenly struck Leland head-on, throwing him up into the air. Hank landed with a thud on the asphalt fifteen feet away, right in front of the fleeing gunmen.

As the van skidded to a stop, Kyle rose to one knee, weapon up. That's when he saw the assault-rifle barrel poking from the driver's-side window. He only had one quick look at the face but it was a woman, and she looked pissed.

He dove behind a whiskey-barrel planter to his left as a flurry of rounds dug into the ground where he'd been only a few seconds ago.

Prone, Kyle brought his M4 around and aimed it at the van. The men had stopped long enough to grab Hank by the arms and were dragging his inert form toward the van.

Kyle fired two quick rounds, aiming high, not wanting to hit Hank, but hoping to force them to let him go.

It worked. They dropped him and piled into the van.

Kyle rolled behind the barrel just as the woman fired another burst, showering him with chunks of the oak barrel. He moved to the left this time, but his own SUV was in his line of fire now, shielding the van as it backed up.

Jumping to his feet, Kyle tried to get a clear shot, but there was a school bus passing by on the street. He couldn't risk it.

Hearing running footsteps behind him, he turned his head and saw Erin Barrett jogging toward him in a crouch, gun down at her side. Her eyes were on Hank.

As the van raced down the street and disappeared around a corner, she ran across the asphalt and knelt by the wounded man. "Hank, don't you dare let them win. You fight and stay here with us!"

Kyle was already dialing 911 when she turned her head to look up at him, fear mirrored on her face.

"Who are you, and why didn't you get here sooner?"

The question threw him for a beat. "I'm an agent with the IRS," he said, using the cover that usually brought questions from the curious to an abrupt stop. "Help will be here soon," he said, coming up to her. "Mr. Leland's still breathing, so he's got a chance, just don't move him. The bleeding isn't bad, but he undoubtedly has broken bones and internal injuries."

She put her hand on Leland's. "I'm here, Hank. Hang on."

He watched her, trying to figure out if she was

a well-placed mole working with terrorists, or the real deal. Until he knew, trusting her was out of the question.

Chapter Two

Erin held on to Hank's hand and continued talking to him. She remembered someone, somewhere, saying that even if you were unconscious you might still be able to hear others.

"You can get through this," Erin repeated, her voice trembling. Desperate to sound as if she believed what she was saying, she cleared her throat and tried again, squeezing his hand very gently. "Don't give up."

As the ambulance arrived and the medical team rushed over, she rose to her feet and stepped back, allowing the EMTs to work. The Navajo man who'd saved her life, shooting the gunman who'd pushed her out into the line of fire, joined her.

"What's your name?" she managed. He was almost a foot taller than her, and his eyes were dark as midnight. They held an intensity that scared her a bit, too, even though she knew she had nothing to fear from him. If it hadn't been for this man, she might have been dead by now.

"I'm Agent Kyle Goodluck, IRS. Who were those people with the guns? Do you know any of them?"

Goodluck… She was alive, and so was Hank at the moment, so maybe he'd lived up to his name. She tried to smile, but the sickeningly sweet scent of blood was making her head spin. "I've never seen them before."

"Did Hank know them?"

"I'm not sure." Seeing him searching the ground, she added, "Did you lose something?"

"I'm hoping to find a cell phone someone may have dropped during the gun battle. Do you have yours and did Hank have one on him?"

"No. Hank said he left his at home, and mine's on my desk. They made me leave it behind."

Fueled by intense fear, her mind was racing. Something about Kyle Goodluck didn't add up. "You said you're IRS, but you came armed…and you've had combat training," she added, struggling to focus. She was so scared she couldn't stop shaking. "I never knew the IRS carried weapons."

"Field agents are usually armed," he said. "Didn't Hank mention I was coming to interview him?"

Seeing her shake her head, he continued. "I was sent to check out some discrepancies in the purchase orders he filed with the Department of Defense." He pulled out his cover government photo

ID, flashed his badge, then quickly placed it all back into his pocket. "If you're worried, the local police will vouch for me."

She wanted to trust this man, after all, he'd saved her life, but something was telling her to hold back. "You don't have to protect me anymore," she said, noticing how closely he stood. "They're gone now."

"For the moment. You've seen these people up close and that makes you a threat to them," he said. "From this point on, expect the unexpected. That's how you'll stay alive."

His bluntness made a chill run up her spine. Agent Goodluck stood straight, shoulders thrown back, a warrior's stance. The black leather jacket enhanced his powerful build. Everything about him spoke of unwavering self-assurance. She didn't know much about Kyle Goodluck, but she had a feeling that this was a man who seldom, if ever, second-guessed himself.

"There's Detective Bowman," Erin said, seeing a familiar face step out of an unmarked SUV. "I remember him from one of the fund-raisers Hank held for the local police. His brother Daniel's in the security business, too."

"I know. They're my brothers," Kyle said.

She blinked, surprised by the revelation.

As her gaze shifted to the EMTs still working on Hank, the full impact of what had happened slammed into her again. Men she'd never seen before had tried to kill her and Hank. One of the gunmen had actually died less than ten feet from her. What was worse, she might still be a target.

Tremors ripped through her and she folded her arms around her middle, as if trying to hug herself.

A heartbeat later, Kyle threw his black leather jacket over her shoulders.

"No, I'm okay," she managed.

"You're holding it together, but that's not the same as okay," he said, his voice gentle.

As Preston came up, he nodded to Erin, then glared at his brother. "Interesting meeting you here so soon after our coffee break. What's the story?"

"A word?" Kyle said, taking Preston aside, but making sure he kept Erin in view.

THEY WERE STANDING less than fifteen feet away from her, but Kyle could see Erin's full attention was on the paramedics getting ready to transport Hank Leland.

"This is part of an NCIS case," Kyle told Preston in a barely audible voice. "I'm here undercover."

"Now tell me something I don't know."

"Earlier this morning Hank Leland called and asked NCIS for help, claiming he was being blackmailed by terrorists. I'd been sent here to monitor Leland's activities anyway, so I was told to go check it out and interview him. Everything looked normal up to the time I pulled into the company's yard, but in a moment, it all went sour," he said. "That's all I have right now, but we're going to need your department's cooperation during my investigation."

Preston nodded curtly. "Why did they come after him here?"

"Don't know. Maybe that was their plan all along. Your guess is as good as mine."

"Leland's company specializes in building safe rooms but that technology isn't classified. What's that got to do with terrorists?"

"Not sure—yet." Kyle glanced around. "Firearms aren't hard to get, so let's begin with explosives and detonators. Does Leland keep any here on site?"

"I'll find out," Preston answered.

"One more thing," Kyle said before he could move off. "I need you to file this as an armed robbery gone bad or something routine like that—not a kidnapping attempt involving probable terrorists. If you need clearance, I can get it for you. I'll also need to keep Erin Barrett in my custody."

"Are you taking over this case? If you are, I'll have to run it through channels."

"Do whatever you have to, and I'll stay with Erin."

As Preston walked off, Kyle saw one of the paramedics block Erin from climbing into the back of the vehicle. "Ma'am, you can't ride in the ambulance with him. We'll transport him to Regional Medical's emergency room and you can meet us there."

As Kyle placed a gentle hand on her shoulder, Erin jumped back and spun around.

"It's okay, Erin, relax. Let the EMTs do their job. Hank's in good hands," he said. "You and I need to talk."

"Hank Leland hired me and gave me a chance— the only one I ever got—and I'm going to make sure he gets the best of care. I'm going to the hospital right now."

"Hank's already getting the care he needs. Your time's better spent answering our questions so we can catch the people who did this to him, and you."

"I'll tell you everything I can—at the hospital," Erin replied, refusing to give an inch.

Preston came up and gave Kyle a brief nod. "Your request has been approved," he said. "I've sent officers to Leland's home to secure the place. I've also sent a deputy to the company's current work site to inform and protect the work crew there." He looked at Erin. "Right now, ma'am, I have to ask you a few questions."

She ran an exasperated hand through her hair. "Everyone wants to talk to me and I get that, but first, I have to make sure Hank's okay. I'm going to the hospital. You can both talk to me there." She looked over at the emergency vehicle heading out the gates. "I have to go."

"All right. My brother can drive you there," Preston said, and saw Kyle nod. "But before you go, could this have been a robbery, maybe for your payroll, or cash on hand?"

Erin shook her head. "No way. If you'd seen them, you'd understand. They were cold and calm, like professionals following a plan. Whatever they wanted, it wasn't cash."

Kyle nodded. He'd seen extremists with the same attitude she'd described. "Come on. I'll take you to the hospital."

KYLE FOLLOWED THE racing emergency vehicle, staying on its tail by taking advantage of the way its flashing lights, horn and siren cleared traffic. At this speed, he couldn't risk more than a glance in Erin's direction, but he was aware of her on almost every level.

She had spirit—the kind that refused to cower or run. Unless he missed his guess, and he seldom did, her courage wasn't the sort that came from training and preparation. It was the deep-seated kind that you were either born with or not.

"So you and Hank are friends?" he asked, running the red light and staying right behind the ambulance, his skill and training in pursuit driving coming in handy now.

"No, not really, but we work together well, and he's a good boss." She hung on tightly to the door handle as he turned left. "He hired me though I had no business experience, and right from the start trusted me to handle the work."

Kyle had no problem believing that. She clearly wasn't the sort who lost it under pressure.

"Hank'll make it through this. He's as tough as they come," she said.

He wasn't sure if she was trying to convince herself or him. "So you're his assistant, right?"

"Officially, I'm the office manager. Sometimes when he's away fulfilling a contract, I run the day-to-day business. When he's here, my job is to make sure things run smoothly."

"Does Leland have any enemies?"

"Not that I know of. Hank always treats his employees and clients fairly."

"You really like him, I gather," he pressed, making another hard right in order to stay close to the ambulance.

She held her breath until they were moving in a straight line again. "I *respect* him."

Kyle kept his eyes on the road. His gut was telling him that there was more to Erin's story, things she was deliberately keeping back. If she was playing a game, he'd see through it fast enough. He was very good at his job, as he'd proven time and time again.

The fox fetish that hung from a leather cord around his neck pressed against his chest, reminding him to stay alert. Fox, a gift from Hosteen Silver, was his spiritual brother, and, according to Navajo tradition, shared its gifts with him. Observation, one of Fox's innate abilities, had become second nature to Kyle. Whether that was because of the fetish or not, he couldn't say, he just knew that it was so.

"Why did your brother suggest I ride with you to the hospital? Was it so you could question me, or is there more to it?"

"You wanted to get there fast, so it made sense for me to give you a lift. Hang on," he added, hitting the brakes and swerving along with the ambulance ahead of him. Its loud air horn blasted. A startled pedestrian wearing white earbuds looked up suddenly, then jumped back onto the curb.

Unsure of which team she was playing on, he intended to be right there when Hank Leland regained consciousness and saw Erin for the first time since the kidnapping attempt. Hank's reaction might be enough to tell him what he needed to know.

"You saved my life, Agent Goodluck, but I don't think I ever thanked you."

"Not necessary. And it's Kyle." He only met those honey-brown eyes for a second, but that's all it took. Just beyond the sadness and fear mirrored there, he saw a gentle vulnerability.

He was a former marine, long ago labeled as a hard-ass, but that never failed to get to him.

He heard the ambulance's air horn just ahead, and a heartbeat later a large black pickup flew into view, running the light, oblivious to the inevitable collision.

"Oh, damn." Kyle hit the brakes and leaned on the horn.

Although he avoided the truck, it was too late for the ambulance. The pickup slammed into its right front end, pushing the emergency vehicle around ninety degrees with a sickening crunch.

Kyle skidded and barely missed clipping the tailgate of the pickup as it fishtailed around in the intersection. Hitting the brakes hard again, he finally managed to stop about fifty feet beyond the crash site. He looked back in the side mirror just as a familiar-looking van drove up and stopped a few feet behind the pickup.

"That idiot just ran the light!" Erin cried out, her voice shaking.

"It wasn't an accident. Get down on the floorboard now," he ordered, grabbing his pistol. "Call 911," he instructed the online computer, not taking his eyes off the van. "Federal officer needs help, GPS location."

"The van! Those are the same men," she said, her voice rising. "Give me a way to fight back."

"Here, defend yourself, but stay down." Kyle

handed her the Glock, then threw open his door, reaching behind the seat for his M4 as he jumped down to the pavement. He'd replaced the magazine with a full load when he put it away, but the thought of a firefight in a city intersection brought him back to his deployments in Afghanistan. Yet here he was in Hartley, New Mexico.

Two men wearing ski masks had already exited the van, both upgunned to assault rifles. They were possibly wearing vests beneath fatigue jackets, too, though he couldn't tell for sure.

As the gunman from the passenger side approached the disabled EMT vehicle, the driver of the van watched the man's flank and front, providing cover. To their right, the pickup driver was limping away from his badly disabled vehicle, pistol in hand. Clearly the collision had crippled his effectiveness.

Kyle advanced to his left, intending on approaching from behind. There was no cover here in the street, but he was sure they were out to nab Hank and were confident that surprise and firepower had put them in control.

The gunman came up to the rear door of the emergency vehicle and rapped on it with the butt of his assault rifle. "Open the door!"

The man's partner, the driver, looked over at Kyle's SUV. Knowing the fight might shift to Erin's position, Kyle moved in.

"Put your weapons down!" Kyle yelled, now partially screened by the van.

Both gunmen whirled instantly, spraying bullets in his direction.

Outgunned for the moment, Kyle dropped to the pavement and rolled left as bullets kicked up chunks of asphalt. He returned fire, but he wasn't alone. As he glanced back, he saw Erin lying flat beside the SUV, firing beneath the engine block at the men's legs.

Both suspects jumped to the driver's side of the van, moving out of view.

Not wanting to shoot in that direction and risk hitting the ambulance beyond, Kyle circled to his left.

The pistol-wielding pickup driver snapped off a few rounds, but shots from the SUV forced him to take cover beside the pickup. Erin had Kyle's back.

Kyle couldn't see the men any more, but he was advancing, weapon up, when the van roared to life. Tires squealing, the vehicle raced backward straight at him. He fired twice, then jumped to his left as the van brushed by him.

Swinging around, prone, he tried to bring his rifle to bear on the van, which had now done a one-eighty and was racing down the street. A bullet screamed past him from behind. Realizing it had come from the pickup's driver, Kyle forgot about the van, rolled and squeezed off three rounds at the driver, who was leaning against his ruined pickup, still shooting.

The shooter flinched, grabbed his side, and slid down the side of the pickup to a sitting position.

Kyle jumped up, weapon aimed at the wounded man, and advanced quickly.

"Drop the weapon now!" he yelled. To his left, he could see an EMT sneaking a quick look out the back door of the unit. "Stay inside!" Kyle ordered.

Kyle was within fifteen feet when the badly wounded man looked directly at him, put the barrel under his chin and shot himself.

Chapter Three

Kyle lowered his weapon and looked away, shaking his head in disgust. A life wasted, just like that. Up to now, he'd only seen that kind of hardcore reaction overseas.

He moved toward the ambulance, put his hand on the door handle, then yelled, "Federal officer. Open up!"

The EMT inside did so quickly, throwing his hands up as the door opened. "Officer, we're not armed, and our patient needs us right now. We've got to keep working, okay?"

Kyle nodded and realized, from the monitor's tone, that Hank had flatlined. As both EMTs worked to revive Leland, one of them talking back and forth with an emergency room doctor through a headset, Erin rushed up. She stood silently beside him, watching.

Minutes passed, the medics working feverishly. After four attempts to restart Leland's heart with the paddles, the one with the headset reported the results, tapped the other EMT on the shoulder, and shook his head. "Call it."

The second medic noted the time and pulled a sheet over the patient's head.

"What are you doing? Don't give up!" Erin demanded.

"Ma'am, his blood pressure bottomed out even before the accident, probably from trauma-induced internal bleeding. Even if we hadn't been stopped here on the street, I doubt he would have made it to the hospital."

She bit down on her lip until it turned white, but when Kyle tried to get closer to comfort her, she stepped away. "I'm fine," she said, though her voice was shaking.

"Everyone here, including us, did everything possible to save him," Kyle said. "Hold to that." His voice was quiet and calm, a tone he'd learned people responded to, and it broke through to her now.

"We might as well go back to the warehouse. There's nothing else we can do here now."

She nodded, and walked back to the SUV with him. Her movements were slow and ponderous as she continued to struggle with what she'd just seen. "I should notify his brother…make funeral arrangements, or at least help with that. I…"

"That'll wait. Right now you need a little time to process what's happened and so do I," he said.

As they climbed into his SUV, he saw her staring ahead, a glassy look in her eyes. Shock. "Seat belt," he said, and she absently complied.

"What I saw today is going to haunt my nightmares for as long as I live," she said after a moment.

Her words touched him. He knew all about things one could never unsee, and memories that refused to die.

"You're right, some things can't be forgotten," he said, his voice nothing more than a deep rumble, "but you'll learn to deal and, in time, the images will come less often."

Kyle started the engine and called his brother on the phone. After a few minutes he ended the connection and glanced at her. "We'll head back to Secure Construction. My brother will wait for us there and he'll want a detailed account of everything that went down."

Ten minutes later, they parked outside the now closed access gates of Secure Construction's fenced compound and waited in the SUV. After several moments a uniformed Hartley police officer came to unlock the gate.

"Have you given any more thought to what these men may have wanted, Erin? You already ruled out cash, but do you keep anything that's dangerous or of high value here, like maybe explosives?"

The person who'd encountered Hank overseas

was said to be a bomb maker with ties to extremists. Firearms were easy to get in the U.S., but finding high explosives was a lot more difficult.

"We use explosives to test the construction of newly designed safe rooms, but we hire out those tests and pick up what's needed en route to the test site. We never really store anything here. There's no need."

Kyle drove into the yard, then pulled up by the main office building, stopping in front of the yellow crime-scene tape. "Don't think—just answer me. What's here that someone would want to steal?"

She didn't hesitate. "Nothing that's worth people's lives." She got out of the SUV and strode to where Preston was standing, waiting for them.

Kyle hung back and watched Erin for a moment longer. She was the picture of courage, but little telltale signs, like the stiff way she was walking and the expressionless look in her eyes told him a different story. Overwhelmed on every level, the human body often adapted and became ultra-calm—almost numb—in order to survive.

If Erin was truly an innocent caught in circumstances she didn't understand, she had his sympathy. This was just the beginning.

ERIN FELT SICK to her stomach. She wanted to curl up into a ball and hide where no one would see her fall apart. Yet the look on Detective Bowman's face told her she had to hold it together for a little bit longer. "You have questions for me, so why don't we go into my office and talk there?" she asked.

"My people are still processing the building so we'll have to talk out here," he said.

"It's okay. I have another smaller office in the warehouse," she said, desperately needing a place to sit down before her knees buckled. "How about we talk in there?"

"Lead the way," Preston said.

She walked to her second office, a cubbyhole on the lower level of the warehouse, near the entrance doors. Detective Bowman and Kyle Goodluck were half a step behind her.

"Detective, Agent Goodluck, please sit down," she said, dropping down into her seat unceremoniously. "Ask me whatever you want, and I'll do my best to answer you, or track down the answers you need."

"How did this whole thing start? Did the three men just burst into the office?" Preston asked.

"I wasn't there when they arrived, I was in here checking out our newest model safe room. We display them with simple furnishings, emergency gear, and supplies to show prospective clients," she said. "After I finished, I went back and saw three men talking to Hank in his office. It all looked like business as usual, so it never occurred to me to ask Joe to stick around a while longer."

"Joe?" Preston asked. "The same guy at the work site? The one I sent a deputy to cover?"

"Yes, Joe Pacheco is our senior construction foreman. You may know him. He's a former police officer."

Preston nodded. "I know Joe. When, exactly, did he and the crew leave?"

"Joe was behind the wheel of one of our big pickups, and pulled out onto the street a few minutes after I sat down at my desk in the main office."

"Who else was on site here at the time?" Preston asked. "Anyone in the warehouse or working in the yard?"

"No, after Joe and the crew left, it was just Hank and me."

"When did you first realize there was trouble?" Kyle asked her.

"After a few minutes, I heard Hank yell at one of the men. I'm better with difficult prospective clients, which is what I figured they were, so I went in to see if I could help calm the situation. That's when I realized all three men were armed."

She took a breath and tried to hold it together. Both men were watching her, but it was Kyle's intense, hooded gaze that got to her. There was something hard and dangerous there. Yet he'd saved her life…. Maybe he was only dangerous to the wrong people.

"What were they arguing about?" Kyle asked.

"They claimed that Hank had double-crossed them. Then one of them pointed his gun at Hank and told him to keep his end of the deal or get ready to die." She shuddered. "I heard that last part just as I walked into the room."

"Describe the men you saw," Preston said.

"The tallest one standing next to Hank was tanned and had a beard. I'd say he stood about six foot one, and was rail thin. The other faces were a blur. I was so scared all I could see were their guns."

"The man who shot himself in the street, was he one of them?" Kyle asked.

"No, I'm pretty sure of that," she answered. "His face was distinctive, even before the…bullet."

"Okay, so there are—were at least four of them. Getting back to earlier now. What happened next?" Preston asked.

"They told us to leave our cell phones, and ordered us outside. They held on to us with one hand, their pistols jammed against our backs," Erin said. "I was sure they intended to kill us, so when I saw you drive into the yard, I elbowed the one behind me in the gut and yelled for help, but he pulled me back again before I could get away. Once we went around the corner of the building, he shoved me out into the open. You know the rest."

She studied their expressions, trying to read them, but their faces were flat, impenetrable.

Preston glanced out the window. "Let's go back to the main office. It looks like my team's finished their preliminary sweep." He reached into his pocket and pulled out a pair of latex gloves. "I'd like you to avoid touching anything, Erin, but wear these in case you forget."

As THEY RETURNED to the main building, Erin could feel her heart hammering. When Preston went to speak to one of the officers standing outside, she focused on Kyle. "This is their case, yet you're taking an active role in the investigation. Is that because he's your brother?"

"No, it's because I'm a federal agent with an interest in what happens here," he answered.

She stared at the floor for a moment, trying not to fall apart. "Hank had been so tense lately. I should have paid more attention."

"Had anything unusual happened lately?"

"Hank never confided in me, but I believe something had been bothering him. It started about a week before he left for Spain. He was tense and short-tempered with everyone, but when he came back, that still hadn't changed."

"Did you ever ask him about it?"

She nodded. "I tried, but he told me that it was family business. That was his way of telling me it was personal and I needed to back off, so I did."

"Family? He wasn't married, right?" Kyle asked.

"I think he meant his brother, Bruce, who works on and off for him."

"Were they close?"

"No. They had nothing in common and could barely stand being around each other. Hank is all about working hard, but Bruce has never been able to hold on to a job for long."

Preston joined them and tossed Kyle a pair of latex gloves. "Okay, we're ready. Let's go inside the main office. I want you to look around carefully, Erin, and tell me if there's anything missing," he said, putting on a set of gloves, too.

"Look for anything that's new, too," Kyle added.

"New, how?" she said. "Are you talking about something he brought back from his trip, like souvenirs, or what's in today's mail?"

"Both," they answered in unison.

Hearing another investigator call his name, Preston said something in a low voice to Kyle.

"Go. I'll handle things here," Kyle said.

As Erin walked inside with Kyle, the first thing that caught her eye was the small plant that lay on the carpeted floor, soil spilling out of its container.

Temporarily forgetting what they'd told her about not touching anything, she picked it up carefully, and scooped the soil back into the pot with a gloved hand.

A second later, she froze. "Oh—I'm so sorry. I didn't think…."

"It's okay. That's why you're wearing gloves. We can't get prints from soil anyway," Kyle said with a gentle smile.

"When the man pushed me out, I bumped into the corner of my desk and knocked over the plant. Considering everything that's happened, it's stupid to worry about this, but if I leave it here, it'll die…too."

Erin turned her face away as tears ran down her cheeks. "Now you're going to think I'm crazy for sure," she managed in a shaky voice. "I held it together through everything—being kidnapped, forced to shoot at someone just to stay alive and seeing three people die. Then I fall apart over this…." Despite all the care she'd lavished on the small desert rose, the plant was still nothing more than a thorny stem with a couple of leaves.

"It's okay," Kyle said, lifting her back to her feet with incredible gentleness. "So how come this little plant means so much to you?" He smiled. "If you don't mind my saying so, it sure doesn't look like much."

She chuckled through her tears. "Hank got it years ago from a client. The original plant had been her great-grandmother's, and the family had a tradition of giving a cutting to people who performed a special service for them. In this case, the woman's husband had passed and she was having a hard time financially so Hank charged her half price for the safe room." She looked at the plant. "There's a legend attached to the desert rose that says it'll only bloom for an owner whose heart has learned to sing."

"And your heart?"

"I guess mine doesn't sing loud enough." She gave him a hesitant smile, then placed the plant in the windowsill next to her desk. "Hank almost killed it, but I took it from him before he could toss it in the trash. Since then, I've done everything I could to make it grow and bloom, but so far nothing."

"I'll speak to my brother, but I'm sure it'll be okay if you want to take it with you."

"Thanks," she said, wiping away her tears with a now muddy, gloved hand. "I can't seem to stop crying, but I'm okay."

He pulled a handkerchief from his pocket and wiped her face. "You're a strong woman, Erin, but you reached your limit. It happens."

"To you?"

"It did—once," he said.

She tried to force herself to swallow so she could stop crying, but her eyes continued to fill with tears. She didn't dare blink.

He placed a hand on her shoulder and gave it a squeeze, but she moved back. "Let's get back to work. Tell me what you need."

"How about a list of company employees, starting with the ones who live here in town?"

"I can access payroll, but I'd have to use my computer. Is that okay? They never touched it."

"Keep your gloves on, but go ahead," he said. As she sat down, he added, "Do you always issue checks to your employees, or do some get paid in cash?"

Her eyes were brimming with tears and it made the numbers on the screen swim but somehow she pulled herself together. "No cash. Most of the money is deposited directly into the employees' bank accounts, but for a few, we still cut checks. Payday is every two weeks—next Friday is the next one," she said, pushing the cell phone she'd left on her desk out of her way as she reached for paper. After loading it into the printer, she looked up at him. "Should I put my cell phone back in my purse?"

"No, that has to stay," he said. "We're still looking for Hank's cell phone, too. You sure it was at his house?"

She stared at her desk, lost in thought. "That's what he told them, but if it's there, it could be anywhere. Last time he lost it, he ended up finding it in his laundry hamper." She paused. "But maybe he didn't go straight home last night after his flight arrived… He has a girlfriend."

"What's her name?" Kyle asked, just as Preston came in.

"Frieda Martinez. He met her about two weeks before he left for Rota, Spain. She was good for him. Though he'd been irritable at work, his whole attitude would change whenever she called. I think he was falling in love with her, not that he would have ever admitted it."

She printed out the complete list of company employees, then handed it to Kyle. "Should I look around inside Hank's office now to see if anything there catches my eye?"

"Go ahead," he said.

"Those are the newest things in here," she said, pointing. On top of Hank's desk were two opened cardboard boxes he'd addressed to himself and mailed here from Spain.

As Kyle came up and took a closer look, he recalled following Hank to a municipal post office in Rota. At the time that had struck him as odd because the base had excellent postal facilities. "Do you know what was inside these?"

She shook her head. "They arrived yesterday, but they were addressed to Hank, so I just set them aside. When I came in this morning they were open, but we never had a chance to talk about it."

Kyle took a pen from his pocket, pulled back the flaps, then stirred up the foam peanuts inside.

She looked over his shoulder. "That's strange. Those are volt meters, but…"

"Looks like they've been gutted, but what did he do with the electronics that were inside them?" Kyle continued to sort through the box. "They're not here. All I see are the outside shells and a few of the metal screws used to hold them together."

"I can't answer that. I don't know," she said.

"Did any of the men who came for him show any interest in these boxes?" Kyle asked.

"No. Their attention was on Hank and me."

In addition to the dismantled volt meters Kyle saw other disassembled plastic and metal electronic devices, including stud finders and other sensors. "Lots of packing material in here just to protect what looks like junk."

"What about that padded envelope?" Preston said, coming in and pointing to the top of the file cabinet.

"That arrived this morning." Out of the corner of her eye, Erin saw Kyle remove a small, familiar-looking cylinder from the shipping box and slip it into his jacket pocket.

Before she could comment, Detective Bowman tore open the envelope and dumped its contents on the desk. Stacks of one hundred dollars bills held together with rubber bands came tumbling out. "Apparently he also mailed this to himself from Spain."

"I have no idea why he'd be mailing cash back home," Erin said. "Of course it's possible he carried the cash over there originally to pay contractors or something... But why mail currency? It would have been easier to just transfer funds from the base to the bank here, or bring it back in his carry-on."

As Preston's phone rang, he hurried back outside. Once alone, Kyle's gaze stayed on her. "If that amount of cash had been withdrawn from his business account, you would have noticed it while balancing the books, correct?"

"That didn't come from any of the accounts I handled," she said.

"It looks to me that there was a part of your boss's business you knew almost nothing about."

All she could do was shrug. "Had you said that to me a few hours ago, I would have told you that you were crazy. Now, I'm just not sure." As another thought suddenly occurred to her, her eyes widened. "The men didn't get whatever it was they were after, and now Hank's dead. What's to stop them from coming back and trying to get answers from me next?"

"Me."

He'd said it without any particular inflection, and that's what made it so scary. That edge of danger, that toughness nothing seemed to pierce, was as much a part of him as the gun he carried on his belt. Yet she'd seen another side of him when he'd realized she was crying. He'd been gentle and kind then, the opposite of the deadly warrior who'd initially come to her aid.

Preston poked his head back into the room. "We've found Leland's cell phone through its GPS chip. Let's move."

"Do you want me to wait here?" she asked Kyle as he was striding to the door.

"No. Stick with us, you'll be safer. We'd also like your help looking through Leland's home."

"But I've only been there a few times. I'm not really familiar with it."

"You still have the advantage over us," Kyle said. "We've never been there. Let's go."

Chapter Four

"A word?"

Kyle recognized Preston's icy tone and knew what was bothering him. Preston seldom missed much. Despite that, he decided to play it out. "What's up?" he asked, stepping away from the SUV.

"Don't give me that bull," Preston growled. "What did you find in the box, and why the hell didn't you turn it over? NCIS has given us the job of processing evidence, and it's not up to you to pick and choose. Are we working together or not?"

"Your department's cooperation is crucial, but I have to treat what I found as classified for reasons of national security. You in?"

Preston nodded.

Putting his latex gloves back on, Kyle pulled the small device he'd found inside the box out of his pocket. "I really doubt there'll be any usable prints on this, except maybe Leland's partial, but based on the markings this is an electrical detonator manufactured in Spain. You can't get hold of something this sensitive in the U.S. without shoveling through a truckload of grief, and maybe not even then."

"So that's why you want to search Leland's place ASAP. You think he shipped detonators hidden in those dismantled electronics and overlooked this one."

"So now we need to find the rest of them," Kyle said.

"How long have you had Hank Leland under surveillance?"

"Since he was spotted in Rota, Spain, meeting with a man on the watch list, a freelance bomb maker with ties to Spanish ecoterrorist groups. That was two weeks ago. I watched him land at the airport last night, get his luggage and pick up his Silverado. After that I followed him to his office. He stayed here for a while, which I suppose is when he unpacked the box, took the tools apart, and found the detonators."

"Where'd he go next?"

"He got into his pickup and headed home, which is ten miles south, off highway 281. He took the old road so I had to give him plenty of room. It was pretty much deserted that time of night, and his house is all by itself out there."

Preston nodded. "I know. I checked. You can spot vehicles for miles."

"Once he got home, he pulled into the garage

and never left again. No other vehicles drove up, either. I maintained surveillance until 3:30 a.m., then drove back into town and checked into the Chamisa Lodge. After catching a few hours' sleep, I returned to his place at 6:00 a.m. There were lights on inside—still no other vehicles—and there was only one set of tracks leading into the property. Leland left for work at seven, and was still there when I went to meet you for breakfast."

"So, let's assume these terrorists are looking for their detonators. What's their target?"

"I don't know and that's a problem," Kyle said.

"Let's go to Leland's house and look around for his cell. We need to find out who he called after his return," Preston said. "I'll also get hold of Joe Pacheco. He's a former police detective, and keeping his eyes and ears open is second nature to him."

"Don't ask him about the detonators directly," Kyle warned.

Preston got the number from Erin and dialed as Kyle walked over to where she was waiting.

"We're still working out a few details," Kyle told her. "We'll leave in a minute."

After his call, Preston motioned Kyle over. "I asked Joe about the type of explosives used by Secure Construction. He said they use a proprietary mix of ammonium nitrate, but they pick it up from Zia Limited as needed. He also said that they use fuses and blasting caps instead of electrical detonators."

"All right, let's get rolling," Kyle said, started to walk away, then stopped and looked back. "Anything on either of the dead kidnappers?"

"Nothing yet. The Office of the Medical Investigator processed their fingerprints, but there's nothing on record—they're ghosts. We're using facial recognition software and running that through the database, and checking with Interpol, but it'll take time. I have a feeling they're foreign nationals—Spanish, most likely, for obvious reasons. The truck they used for the hit on the ambulance was stolen and they avoided cameras at that intersection. One more thing. The one who shot himself…those bruises on his face predated his death by at least a week. That's based on the medical investigator's preliminary report."

"Get Daniel up to speed on this. He's got clearance," Kyle said.

Daniel Hawk, their foster brother, owned the largest security firm in the Four Corners. Level One Security protected more than half the high profile businesses and state government installations in Northern New Mexico.

"Once we identify the terrorist group we're dealing with, Daniel may be able to suggest possible targets in this area—facilities or personnel," Kyle said.

"Good plan."

"I'll take Erin over to Leland's house. Let's see if on the way there, I can get her to tell me something we don't already know."

THOUGH KYLE'S GAZE was on the road ahead, he was aware of everything about the woman beside him. Erin intrigued him. She accepted her own vulnerabilities instead of trying to conceal her fears, and held it together when it mattered.

Hearing the incoming-call tone, Kyle glanced at the phone display and saw Preston's name. He connected the call and said, "I'm here."

"I just got a report from the officer watching Leland's residence. Someone drove up and slipped inside through the back. I told the officer to wait for backup unless the suspect gets back into his vehicle and tries to leave."

Kyle pressed down on the accelerator. "Back up your officer and cover the rear. I'll take the front and block the driveway."

After he ended the call, he glanced over at her. "When we get there, stay inside the SUV and duck down. This thing is built like one of your safe rooms, and no one can get in once it's locked."

"IRS, huh? I don't think so," she muttered. "Who are you, really?"

"Your best friend while this investigation is ongoing."

"That doesn't answer my question."

"You saw my badge and you know the Hartley P.D. trusts me. That's all you need." He made a hard left that had her groping for the armrest.

"How long have you lived in this area?" he asked Erin as they were forced to slow down almost to a crawl. Up ahead, several steers had wandered up to the shoulder and were eating tall grass fed by runoff. Two ranchers were busy trying to get the animals back through an open gate into a pasture.

"Practically all my life," Erin answered. "There's plenty of work, with all the oil and gas companies. I earn a decent salary, so with luck, in a few years I'll have the stake I need."

"To do what?" He moved to the right shoulder, eased past the men and the cattle, then was able to pick up speed again.

She sat back in her seat, adjusting to the sudden acceleration.

"I'm going to buy some decent farmland and grow chiles," she said. "I've got a green thumb, and love getting my hands dirty and working with the soil. Farming…that's my dream. One day it'll be more than that—it'll be a fact."

There'd been no wavering and, for a moment or two, she'd reminded him of himself. He'd worked hard to get to where he was. Nothing had ever come easy, but he'd stuck to his dream and achieved what he'd set out to do. He had a feeling she would, too.

"Hang on!" Kyle made a sharp turn to the right off the highway, through an open gate and down a gravel lane.

Her eyes widened. "Are you trying to kill us?"

"Relax, I've got this."

"And you expect me to believe you're an accountant? Sure, and there's a glacier in that arroyo over there," she grumbled.

He didn't answer, but slowed even further as the road narrowed into a pothole-ridden pathway. Ahead, he could see the fading rooster tail of dust trailing behind Preston's vehicle.

Kyle slid to a stop behind the Ford pickup, which had been backed up and parked in front of the garage, its tailgate next to the overhead door.

"He's blocked off now. Grab my keys out of the ignition, and lock up," Kyle said, jumping out.

She reached for the keys just as he shut the door.

Hand on the butt of his holstered weapon, Kyle raced toward the front porch in a crouch, looking through the windows of the single-story ranch-style home. If anyone opened the garage door, he'd hear it and turn back.

Stepping silently onto the porch, he opened the screen door, then reached for his lock pick.

Just then he heard a click and the door swung

open. Kyle found himself face-to-face with a big man wearing sunglasses and a baseball cap.

Kyle slipped halfway inside before the intruder could shut the door. Pinned for a second, Kyle gave it all he had and shoved. As the heavy door flew open, the man stumbled backward across the foyer. He bounced off a small deacon's bench and fell to the floor, losing his sunglasses.

The intruder recovered quickly, scrambling to his feet and racing toward a door just beyond the kitchen area.

That door suddenly opened and Preston moved in, another officer right behind him.

"Damn." The man ducked left toward a long hall.

Kyle dove across an easy chair and tackled the big guy waist-high. They both fell to the floor of the hall, Kyle on top.

"Police!" Preston yelled, running over. "Give it up!"

Kyle pinned the guy's arms and placed his forearm at the man's throat. Up close now, with no sunglasses and the intruder's cap lost in the struggle, the face looked eerily familiar.

As the uniformed officer moved in and placed the man in handcuffs, Preston read him his rights. He then checked the man's wallet for an ID. "You're Bruce Leland, Hank's brother?"

"Yeah, and I've got a right to be here. Call

Hank, he'll tell you. Get these cuffs off me before I press charges."

Preston nodded to the officer, and as Bruce was uncuffed, Kyle focused on the man's face. The photo on file looked much younger, but it was the same man.

"Bruce!" Kyle heard Erin's voice behind him.

Kyle glanced at her. "I told you to stay in the SUV."

"Once I saw the window sticker for casino parking, I realized who you were chasing." She glared at Bruce. "What do you think you're doing, breaking into your brother's house?"

"I just came to return that power drill," he said, gesturing to the one next to a bookcase under construction. "I didn't have my keys, but I remembered Hank told me that all the back door needed was a credit card in the lock and a good shove."

Kyle glanced at the drill, noting the handle was dusty. From the looks of it, it hadn't been touched in weeks.

Bruce gave Erin a quizzical look. "What are *you* doing here, Erin? Don't tell me you saw my pickup and called the cops?"

"No," Erin said, but before she could say more, Kyle interrupted.

"We need to speak to you, Mr. Leland."

"Who's *we?*" he asked, fear making his voice rise. Preston flashed his badge, and Kyle did the same.

"You've got a gold badge," he said, looking at Kyle. "What are you, FBI?"

Kyle didn't answer. "We need to search your truck. You can give us permission or we can get a warrant while you remain in custody. Your choice."

"Go ahead, search all you want." He looked back at Erin. "What's going on?"

"Mr. Leland, we have some bad news for you about your brother," Preston said.

Kyle saw the fleeting, panicked look Bruce gave Erin. Maybe they were both involved in what was happening. Hadn't she mentioned needing money for her future?

Too many questions, not enough answers. He intended to fix that—and soon.

Chapter Five

As Preston gave him the news, Bruce, now standing, swayed slightly then caught himself. "Murdered? That can't be..." he said, shaking his head.

Preston gave him the details.

Bruce clamped his mouth shut so tightly, his lips turned pale. "This has something to do with you, doesn't it," he said, glaring at Erin. "My brother trusted you, but you're still alive and he's dead?" He stared at her, as if trying to process the unthinkable. "What kind of trouble did you get him into?"

"I had nothing to do with what happened to your brother," she snapped.

He gave her a disgusted look, then glanced at Preston and Kyle. "Look at her, she's beautiful. Erin had my brother under her thumb. Hank was a good man. Nobody would want to hurt him," he argued. "Not so much with Erin. She's the one who decides who gets a raise and who doesn't, she hires and fires. If anyone has enemies, it's her."

Kyle watched them with interest. As the two of them finally lapsed into an uneasy silence, he spoke. "You had that much influence at the company, Erin?"

"There's no way my job had anything to do with what happened!" she said, glaring at Bruce. "This was never about me," she added, appealing to Kyle, then Preston. "I told you, their attention was on Hank this morning. I just…got in the way."

"And made things worse, no doubt," Bruce said. "What'd you do, piss them off even more?"

"You think Ms. Barrett was involved?" Preston asked. "If so, what's your explanation for the second kidnapping attempt, the one where your brother's ambulance was ambushed on the way to the hospital?"

Bruce tried to sit, but his legs suddenly buckled and he fell down onto the sofa cushions with a dull *whomp.* "I don't know. Finish the job they started?

"You're a federal cop," Bruce continued after a beat, looking at Kyle. "My brother just came home after spending two months in Spain. What are you really, CIA?"

"No, I'm not CIA," Kyle answered. "That agency has no directive to work within the U.S."

"So then you're FBI or Homeland Security."

"I'm a federal agent investigating some business irregularities that track back to your brother, among other things," Kyle said. Bruce seemed to accept his answer, but as he glanced at Erin, he could see the open skepticism on her face.

"Agent Goodluck is currently coordinating his investigation with the Hartley Police Department," Preston added.

"So now what?" Bruce said. "Am I under arrest?"

"You're free to leave—after you give your statement," Kyle said. "In addition to explaining what you were doing here, we'll need you to account for your whereabouts during the past twenty-four hours."

"What about me?" Erin said. "Am I free to go?"

"No, sorry. I'll need you to stick with me a while longer," Kyle said.

As Bruce left the room with the uniformed officer, Erin shook her head. "Hank was nothing like his brother," she said, "but in all fairness, I seem to bring out the worst in Bruce."

"Why's that?" Kyle asked.

"Hank set it up so Bruce had to go through me to get to him. Bruce couldn't con me, so my job was to screen his visits and keep him at bay unless it was absolutely necessary that Hank speak to him."

"Okay, have a seat. I'll be right back." Kyle went to the back room where Preston was looking around. Standing in the hall so he could keep his eye on Erin, he spoke softly. "NCIS obtained a warrant and placed some listening devices in this house. A team took care of that a few days before I arrived in town."

"Have you listened to the audio?"

"No, not yet, but others in the agency have," he said, "I'm going to check with my bosses right now, so I'd like you to keep an eye on Erin for me."

Kyle went outside and pulled out his satellite phone from his jacket pocket. A few moments later, he got the answer he expected, but before he could end the call, his supervisor, Martin Hamilton, got on. He wasn't happy.

"All I've heard is bad news. What have you got so far, Agent Goodluck?"

He gave his boss the short version. "I'm on the trail, sir, but I've been back less than twenty-four hours."

"Yet you've already got three bodies stacked up, including a naval reserve officer who was clearly in trouble up to his ass," he said. "We need answers."

"Yes, sir, I'll be in touch." Kyle muttered a curse as he went back into the house.

As he entered, Preston was shaking his head. "There's nothing of interest here, except an expensive strand of pearls, a present meant for Frieda Martinez, based on the attached card."

"Frieda mentioned wanting a strand and he decided to buy it for her, though personally I thought it was much too soon for that kind of gift," Erin said, coming over.

"I'm getting the idea you didn't like Frieda," Kyle observed.

"No, it's not that. Like Hank, I barely knew her." She paused, then continued. "There's something you should know about Hank. Business was good, and for the first time in years, Hank was bored and restless. Then he met Frieda and his whole attitude changed. He was crazy about her, but as I said, they'd only known each other for a few weeks."

Kyle listened carefully. To him, Hank was beginning to sound like a man going through a midlife crisis and looking for excitement. Maybe that's how he'd been recruited. Money wasn't always the motivator.

"Did you ever meet Frieda face-to-face?" Kyle asked.

"Yeah, a few times when she came to the office to meet Hank for lunch," Erin answered.

"And?" Kyle pressed.

"She was polite to me, but not friendly."

"Any chance she's from Spain?"

"I don't know. She has a faint accent, something I associate with English as a second language, but that's all I can say for sure."

"Preston, get an address on her, then let's go talk to her," Kyle said and saw his brother nod.

"Erin, I'd like you to come in with us, too. Seeing a familiar face, one Hank trusted, might help."

"Okay."

Kyle led her toward the door, sticking close to her side. Until he knew for sure whether Erin was his best asset, or an enemy, he should keep her under guard; he wouldn't let her out of his sight.

THEY WERE ON their way moments later. "Nice, safe speed," she said. "I was beginning to think that driving under eighty miles per hour wasn't part of your M.O."

"Cop speak?" he asked, grinning.

"Hey, I watch TV," she said. She was silent for several long moments, then finally spoke again in a heavy voice. "There's something I still don't get. You pulled into Secure Construction just as those men were attempting to kidnap us. That wasn't a coincidence. I think you were expecting trouble, but if that's true, why didn't you come sooner, before it could go that far?"

"I went over as soon as I got the call to interview Hank. I had no way of knowing what was going to happen. I think the only person that wasn't taken by surprise was Hank."

"Maybe so," she answered in a quiet voice. "I thought I knew Hank, but this.… Maybe nobody ever knows anyone," she added, looking directly at him. Despite the steadiness of his gaze, there was a barrier there, a point where the proverbial shutters came down and she wasn't allowed to see past. He was ostensibly one of the good guys, but it was hard to trust someone who clearly didn't trust her.

"Do we have a problem?" he asked, as if he'd read her mind.

"Maybe. I want to trust you, Kyle, but you're not who you say you are, and you're keeping things from me. When someone else decides what I should and shouldn't know, that makes me nervous."

"It shouldn't. I'm on your side. You've seen that already."

"You say you're keeping me with you so you can protect me, but if I'm in danger, why aren't we holed up in some safe place?"

"Your best bet is to stay on the move with me. I'm not in a position to trust anyone else with your safety, except my brothers, and they have their own work to do right now. If you're with me, you might also see something that jogs your memory, a detail that could be important. You've been working with Hank for quite a while."

"I'm not connected to whatever mess Hank was in. I work hard, and my long-term goals have nothing to do with violence, control, or whatever these killers are after. I want to make a living farming the land. Check my background, and you'll see I'm exactly who I say I am."

"Whether you like it or not, you're involved, and you can't reason with these people, or fight them alone. You need me. I'm good at what I do, and I'll keep you safe."

"What happens tonight? Once you drop me off at home, I'll be on my own anyway."

"You can't go home. Not yet. I can't just put an officer near your door and hope for the best."

"You think that the men who killed Hank have someone inside the police department?" she asked, reading between the lines.

"I don't know, so I'd be gambling with your life. As far as my not being completely open with you," he added, "in my job, everything is on a need-to-know basis."

"I suppose that explains why you took something from the box on Hank's desk and put it in your pocket without telling anyone, including the police." Although she knew what it was, for now, she'd say nothing.

"I gave it to Preston when he and I were alone. He'll sign it over to my brother Daniel who has the security clearance needed to find out what we need to know. I also sent a photo of it to my boss."

"There's a whole lot more to that story, but okay—for now."

"Take me at face value." Kyle gave her a disarming smile. "I'm your bodyguard."

Her skin prickled with awareness. Kyle was high voltage excitement, a force of nature, adventure waiting to happen. Danger clung to him like an unholy aura. Considering that she was in a life-or-death fight, staying with Kyle was her best option.

"I'm really not bad company," he said, his eyes dancing.

Her heart began beating overtime. "I'm sure you've got a long list of women who love spending time with you. Things are always happening when you're near. It's like a wild roller coaster ride, periods of calm are just the prelude to the next spiraling downturn."

"That's quite a compliment."

"I don't like roller coasters, I like paddle boats."

"Up to now," he said with a playful grin, then pulled to the side of the road and parked just to the right of a small cottage. "Okay, this is it. We're here."

"What a beautiful little casita. Frieda's got good taste," she said.

Freshly watered red and yellow miniature roses, covered in their last big blooms of the season, bordered the path to the door and glistened in the late afternoon light. As she walked up the narrow sidewalk, Erin relaxed, more concerned now about keeping her shoes dry and avoiding the small puddles on the concrete.

As she glanced at Kyle, she could see the tension in his body. He kept looking from window to window, his hand on the butt of his pistol. His reaction seemed out of place. "Frieda's already met me, so why don't you let me introduce you?"

"Fine," he said, in a clipped tone.

"Frieda, it's me, Erin," she called out as they reached the front porch. Erin knocked on the front door, and as she did, it creaked open about an inch.

Kyle suddenly grabbed her by the waist and pulled her away. "Stay back. *Don't* touch anything!"

Chapter Six

"You think there's a burglar inside?" Erin whispered, startled and trying to catch her breath.

"No, I think the door's wired." Kyle examined the locking mechanism, then leaned forward and sniffed the air. "I smell sulfuric acid. Get behind the SUV and stay low. There's a bomb inside."

"Should I call the bomb squad?"

"No. Do *not* make any phone calls. You might trigger something. Just hang tight, I'm going in through the back," he said, then jogged down the side of the house and disappeared around the corner.

She stayed behind the SUV for five of the longest minutes of her life, watching the house through the windows. Then the front door slowly opened.

"It's safe now," he called out. "I disarmed the device by separating the chemicals, but circle around and come in through the back door anyway."

Erin headed across the damp lawn, trembling

hands jammed into the pockets of her slacks. Her shoes were getting wet, but that touch of normality became a welcome distraction. Her entire world was spinning out of control. Every time she took a breath, something bad seemed to happen.

Kyle was waiting for her at the back door and let her into a small kitchen.

Erin looked around. Everything was nicely arranged and clean, but it looked like a model home, or one listed for sale—impersonal and without a soul.

She expelled her breath in a low hiss. "Yesterday, my life was so completely normal—water the plants before going to work, eat breakfast, clean up, go to the office, come home, fix dinner, check the garden. I had my routines worked out so I could fit everything in. It was perfect."

He stared at her as if she'd begun speaking in a foreign language. "*That's* your idea of perfect?"

"For me, it is. Life is complicated enough, always throwing curveballs and putting up barriers to keep you from where you want to go. That's why I try to anticipate everything, so I can always be prepared. Now, things that make no sense are happening minute by minute. Like this," she said, waving toward the front door. "Someone wanted to blow up this beautiful cottage. Do you think this is connected to the people who went after Hank and me?"

"My guess—yes," he said, leading the way into the living room. "Give me a minute. I need to call my brother."

Erin remained where she was and listened in.

"I found a crude but generally effective incendiary device," he said. "There was a container of what looked to be potassium chlorate and sugar, along with a vial of sulfuric acid. That would generate intense heat once they combined. Add to that the bottle of camp-stove fuel only a few inches away. Had we pushed the door open enough to step inside, the acid would have spilled, setting off a real inferno," he said, then walked to the hearth. "From what I see here, someone, probably Frieda Martinez, burned some papers in the fireplace. From the scent, lighter fluid was the accelerant."

With a gloved hand, he reached into the soot-filled mess. "There's a driver's license that's melted pretty bad, but I can still make out most of the numbers," he said, and read them off. "I've got most of the photo, too. Hang on." He snapped a picture of it with his phone camera, and pressed a few icons. "I've just sent it to you. Call me back once you have more on Martinez. She's cut her hair real short since this photo was taken, but I caught a glimpse of her behind the wheel during the kidnapping attempt and the photo is a good match. I'm guessing she was also driving the van when the ambulance was attacked."

Several minutes later, Preston called Kyle back. Kyle set the phone down on the table, putting it on speaker as he searched the room.

"Bad news," Preston said. "With the exception of her address, the rest of the personal information that was on the license is pure fiction. Since you wanted me to keep things low key, I've asked Daniel to look into this. Our brother Paul's working there, too. He's a major tech geek so you'll have more information soon."

"Good. That's backup I can trust."

"Gene's also available if we need manpower, but for now he's at the ranch," Preston said. "Speaking of using backup, you shouldn't have tried to disable that device on your own. We have specialists who deal with that kind of thing."

"I'm trained to disarm IEDs and incendiary devices that the local bomb squad has probably never even seen," he said. Stepping over to a desk near the corner, but not touching anything, he continued. "I think Frieda took a laptop with her. I can see a faint dust outline on the desk."

Erin followed Kyle down the hall to the bedrooms. He'd picked up the cell phone and turned off the speaker so she couldn't hear what was being said. She glanced around Frieda's bedroom. There were no knickknacks, or plants, or personal items that might reveal something about her.

The second he ended the call, Erin cleared her

throat. "I know you have a plan, and I'd like to know what that is."

"What I do next depends on what happens now. At the moment, I'm looking for any kind of lead. Try to relax," he said, continuing his search.

"Relax? Are you crazy? People want to kidnap me, my boss was murdered, and although it may seem trite, it's nearly six and I haven't had anything to eat all day." She almost cringed. "I can't believe I just said that."

He gave her a gentle smile. "I've pushed you too hard and haven't given you a chance to process things. I'm sorry, Erin," he said. "Stick with me just a while longer, then we'll go get something to eat."

"Let me go home, please, even if it's just for a little bit. I can do normal things there, and after that, maybe I'll be able to think straight."

"That's too big a risk. I'll take you somewhere safe, and we'll pick up dinner on the way. A full stomach and sleep can make all the difference in the world."

"No way I'm sleeping tonight. I'm just too keyed up."

"By the time we get to the safe house, and you've had down time, it'll come naturally."

"Maybe," she said, still unconvinced.

He looked around the room one last time, then took her back out to the SUV. "We know Frieda has been working to change her looks. Her hair is now very short. Next, she'll probably change the color, or wear a wig. I only got a quick look at her, so as it stands now, I'd have trouble picking her out of a lineup. Do you think you'd still be able to recognize her?"

"Yes. There's one thing Frieda can't change. I think she broke her nose at one point, and it left a bump that isn't unattractive, but it's impossible to hide."

"Good to know," he said, then smiled as they got underway. "See that? You're already getting the hang of it. Before we're through, you might decide to open your own P.I. firm."

She stared at him, wondering if he'd lost his mind.

He laughed. "Your problem is that you want to operate from an itinerary, and criminal investigations don't work that way."

"I like structure. If you really do work for the government, you have rules and procedures you have to eventually follow, too. Without direction— knowing where you're going and what you have to do—all you have is confusion."

"I do have a process, but it's not set in stone. When I'm on the trail, I follow whatever leads turn up. So far my only one is Frieda Martinez. I saw a waitress uniform in her closet, and a matchbook from the Quarter Horse Bar on her nightstand."

"I missed that," she admitted.

"Okay, let's focus on what you did see."

"I wasn't searching for anything specific. I was watching you and waiting for you to finish speaking to your brother."

"You were still there, and while you were waiting, you were also glancing around," he said. "Think back."

"The bed was unmade, the closet door open and there were a few days' worth of dirty clothes on the floor along with a couple of pairs of shoes. Two pairs of shoes? Every woman I know has more than four pairs. Also, there were no plants, stuffed animals or little decorator touches anywhere. I found that strange. Most women like to surround themselves with the things that make a house a home."

"Good observations," he said. "What else?"

"The calendar. Some of the days had penciled-in dots. There was one on the first Monday of the month, then another on the following Thursday."

"See that? You're aware of more details than you realize."

"Maybe so, but that doesn't tell us anything. I sure wish I could think of *something* that would make these people crawl back under whatever rock they came from."

"Experience tells me not to expect easy answers. Stay alert. Any change, like the calendar details you spotted, may eventually tell us something important."

Erin had hated change as far back as she could remember, but she'd always consoled herself with the thought that it eventually brought something good. This time she couldn't envision any way that could happen.

He reached over and placed his hand over hers. It was hard, calloused and strong, but his touch was gentle. "You'll get through this, Erin. I'm a good judge of character, and you're tougher than you realize."

"I'm strong and I can take care of myself, but this…"

"Is why I'm here," he answered.

She glanced out the window. He was so sure of himself, it was tempting to let go of caution and just lean on him. She'd seen him fight and knew he was a formidable adversary.

Yet even though they were on the same side, when she looked at him, she saw a more immediate danger. She was drawn to Kyle, even though she knew the attraction was foolish and downright dangerous.

Kyle reminded her of the hollyhock plant that had blown into her yard a few months ago, probably pulled up as a weed from a neighbor's property. She'd tried to cultivate it, but it never developed the roots it needed to survive the wind storms that followed. One morning she'd discovered that it had been swept away.

After Kyle found the answers they both needed, he'd also be gone without a trace. It was the nature of his job, and of a man who would choose that profession.

KYLE KNEW PRESTON would soon be taking prints at Frieda's house and looking for hair and other trace evidence. With Daniel's help, maybe they'd be able to come up with her real name.

"We're going to the Quarter Horse Bar?" Erin asked, bringing Kyle's thoughts back to the present.

"Yes. I want to ask the bartender about Frieda. While I'm talking to him, I'd like you to keep watch. If you see her, or if you think someone else is watching us, let me know right away. I'll take it from there."

While parking near the bar's smaller side entrance, he noted that the lot was less than half full.

"Our timing's just right. It's not so crowded the bartender won't have a few minutes to spare. Stay beside me."

Moments later, they walked across the dimly lit room. Kyle flashed his badge as the bartender came over. "I'm looking for an employee of yours, Frieda Martinez."

"She should have been here an hour ago. If you see her, tell her she's fired," the man spat out.

"Are you the owner?"

"Nah, I just manage the place. My name's Ed Huff, detective."

Kyle didn't bother to correct him. If Huff thought he was with the local P.D., so be it.

"Tell me more about Frieda. Does she hang out with anyone special, customers or staff?"

"Like everyone else, she seems to have her favorites," he said. "So why are the police suddenly interested in her?"

"We need to ask her a few questions, that's all." He brought out two photos—one of Bruce and another of Hank Leland. "Either of these men look familiar?"

"Yeah, that's Bruce Leland and that's his brother Hank," he said, pointing. "They're both regulars— Bruce more so than Hank. Hank's been gone for a while, some overseas business, but Bruce is here almost every night. In fact, Bruce introduced Hank to Frieda. From what I could tell, Frieda and Hank really hit it off."

Ed signaled another employee. "Alex, take over!" he called out, then glanced back at Kyle. "Come to my office."

Instead of following them, Erin pointed to a vending machine a few feet down the hall. "Would you excuse me for a moment? I need some quick energy."

"Go ahead," Kyle said.

Ed led the way into a tiny, cramped office. "The employee files are here, but since we have a high rate of turnover, we keep application forms short and simple. No one here is big on paperwork."

Ed pulled out a manila file folder with a hand-lettered tab and dropped it on the desk. "There you go, detective. That's everything I've got."

Kyle studied its contents. As Ed had promised, the file contained only a one-page application which listed Frieda's known address and last job as an inventory specialist for Zia Limited. The company sounded familiar, then he remembered why.

"I'm sick and tired of dealing with her, so Frieda's going to be looking for a new job."

"Don't let me be the one responsible for that. All I've got is a few questions for her. Hank Leland was killed this morning."

Ed's eyes grew wide. "That's terrible news, Hank dead. That's probably why she never showed up for work. What the heck happened? If you officers are asking questions, it wasn't just an accident, was it?"

"I'm afraid not," he said. "I just need to ask Frieda what she knows about the Leland brothers."

"She might be able to help," he agreed. "She's real outgoing with the customers, especially the guys."

"I've never met her, so tell me. What makes Frieda so easy to talk to?"

"Frieda just draws you in. She's got beautiful green eyes and copper hair that shines like silk. You get what I'm saying?"

"Yeah, she's hot."

"Scalding, and she knows it. Frieda would have never given Bruce Leland the time of day unless she'd had an angle. Bruce is a loser so I'm betting she used him to meet Hank. Frieda strikes me as someone with a lot of street savvy, a woman who plans to be rich someday."

Hearing a commotion in the hall, Kyle glanced out the open doorway. A tall, muscular man in baggy slacks and a tight green T-shirt was standing inches from Erin, his hands on her, pressing her shoulders against the wall.

Kyle flew across the gap that separated them. Grabbing one of the man's arms, he twisted it around, and shoved him face first against the wall. "You have a problem with her—you have a problem with me."

Ed hurried over. "Bubba, what the hell are you doing back here? You know this area's employees only."

A tall, flashy redhead in tight slacks and blouse stepped up. "It's my fault, Ed. I came in to pick up my check and brought Bubba with me. When this woman reached for my arm, Bubba maybe thought she was trying to rough me up or steal my purse."

"I'm sorry I gave you the wrong impression," Erin said, catching her breath. "I thought you were someone else."

Kyle eased up on the big man's arm, letting him turn around. "I'm going to let you go, dude, but keep your hands off the ladies or you'll find yourself in handcuffs."

Bubba rose to full height and stared down at Kyle with fire in his eyes.

"Guess you thought I was Frieda didn't you?" the red-haired woman said with a wry smile. "I'm Rosalie, the taller one. Bubba's had my back since last week, when a guy out in the parking lot came up from behind and grabbed my arm. He thought I was Frieda too until he saw my face. From the back we get mistaken for each other all the time."

"Did you recognize the man who tried to grab you?" Kyle asked her.

"I've seen him around, so I guess he's a customer, 'cause he sure doesn't work here," Rosalie said. "He was pissed off at Frieda, grumbling about her not playing by the rules, or some such bull. Just about the time he realized I wasn't her, Bubba jumped in and hammered him with a couple of punches to his face."

"I'm really sorry I startled you," Erin said.

The young woman smiled. "It's fine. I'm sorry,

and so's Bubba," she said. Looking directly at her friend, she added, "Apologize."

"Yeah, sure. It was a mistake, that's all," Bubba responded.

"Let's go," Kyle said.

Once outside the bar, Kyle glared at her. "You decided to approach a woman you thought was Frieda all by yourself? What were you thinking? What if she'd pulled a gun?"

"I was afraid she'd get away the second I called out to you."

"Do *not* do anything like that again," he growled. "You're with me because you saw at least one of the remaining kidnappers up close. The other ones have no way of knowing if you can provide a link to them or not, so you're in their sights, too."

"The longer I stick with you, the more they're bound to think I know more than I do."

"Maybe, but I stand between you and them. All things considered, you're better off following my game plan."

"Yeah, I get that, but I don't want to be dead weight, either. By helping you, I'll be helping myself. I'm going to take a more active role."

"How exactly do you plan to do that?" he asked, biting off each word.

"For one, I'm going to keep my eyes open, like I did just now at the Quarter Horse Bar, and take action if necessary—within reason, of course," she added. "You should start adapting your tactics and figuring out ways to use my help more effectively. If you don't, I'll just have to get creative."

"So now you've got a death wish?"

"No, just the opposite. The sooner you find answers, the faster I'll get back to my—" She stopped speaking abruptly, and looked away.

"What?"

"My life…but there's no going back to the way things were, not ever," she said in a heavy voice. "For starters, I'm probably jobless. Hank's the sole owner of the company and now that he's gone, I'll have to call his attorney to find out what the company's status is. Will the doors stay open so we can wrap things up? We've got work contracted out and employees that'll need to be paid."

"You'll be able to contact the lawyer once we're in a secure location and the call can't be traced."

"Hank trusted me. I can't just walk away and leave things in chaos. I have to finish whatever needs to be done."

Despite the fact that her job may have come to a close, and that responsibility could now lie in the hands of another, she still wanted to see things through. It was clear to him that she found comfort in rules, even self-imposed ones. Yet predictability of any kind could be her downfall.

"I hear you," he said, as they got back into the SUV.

He remembered Hosteen Silver's teachings. To restore order, you first had to find the pattern, he'd say. The first step was identifying what didn't fit within the framework of harmony.

As he considered it, Kyle realized he'd been going about things wrong. To find answers, he had to start with what now stood at the center of the chaos—Erin Barrett.

Chapter Seven

As Kyle pulled out into the street, a white van, parked against the curb, started up, did a one-eighty, and nearly got hit by an oncoming car. The other driver, who'd had to stand on his brakes to avoid a collision, honked loudly.

"The crazy driver in that van could have killed someone! The jerk's probably drunk. We have way too many DWIs around here," Erin said.

Or the guy is stone sober but real anxious to follow us. On his guard now, Kyle decided to play it out.

"There's also a chance we're being followed," he said, looking in the rearview mirror.

"You're talking about that same van, the one with the electrical company sign on the side?" she asked.

"Yeah, the suspects we're dealing with seem to prefer vans, and that sign's magnetic and easy to slap on."

Using the SUV's voice recognition capability,

he spoke clearly. "Search Consolidated Electric," he said, and waited for the computer to complete its task.

"No business by that name is listed in Hartley. Closest match—Denver," came the disembodied reply.

"Your instincts were right. Can we turn the tables on the driver?" she asked.

"Maybe." A high-threat environment was never an easy thing to deal with, but Erin was adapting quickly. "Let me get some backup first.

"Call Preston," Kyle told the computer as he checked the rearview mirror again for the van. The vehicle had changed lanes and was behind them now, about ten car lengths back. It appeared to be pacing them.

"Pres," he said, "I'm being followed by a white van with a Consolidated Electric sign on the driver's door. Can you get behind him?"

"What's your current location?" Preston asked.

"Erin and I are headed east on Crestview, next cross street is Twenty-first."

"Okay. Take Twenty-first south, but try to get caught by the red light so I can have some time to catch up. I'm at the taco place west on Fourteenth having dinner, but can probably reach Twenty-first in five. If the van drops off, let me know."

"Copy," Kyle said.

"It's still back there," Erin said, glancing into the side mirror.

Kyle managed to go slow enough to catch the next red light.

Straight ahead past the intersection, he noted that Crestview Mall was busy this evening.

As he began the right turn onto Twenty-first with the van two car lengths away, he saw red-and-blue flashing lights coming up Crestview, heading in their direction.

Erin saw the squad car at the same time. "Is that Preston? Not very subtle, is he?"

"It's not me, dammit. It's a uniform answering an emergency call," Preston's voice came from the speaker. "Just act normal and hope your tail doesn't panic."

Suddenly the van sped up. It raced through the intersection and pulled into the mall's parking lot.

"He spooked!" Erin said, turning in her seat.

"He went past Twenty-first into the mall parking lot," Kyle informed his brother. "Hang on, Erin!" Kyle slipped into the inside lane, hit the brakes, then whipped into the mall lot.

"There's the van and it's on the move!" Erin said, pointing. "He's headed for the theater parking area."

"I see him," Kyle said, circling around the outside perimeter. "East side, Preston," he called out.

"I'm making the turn onto Twenty-first now,"

Preston replied. "I'll head for the back of the theater and cut him off."

Kyle had to slow down for a group of teenagers gathered around a car, then lost visual.

"There's the van!" Erin said a second later, pointing to the curb alongside the massive building. "The driver's getting out and running for the entrance."

"Good eye!" Kyle replied. He raced down a line of parked cars and pulled up alongside the van.

Erin jumped out as soon as the SUV came to a stop. "Hurry, before we lose him in the crowd."

"Wait!" Kyle yelled, grabbing the phone and sliding out of the vehicle.

He stopped by the van, and looked inside. The keys weren't in the ignition, and the vehicle was unoccupied. Taking out his pocket knife, he quickly punctured a tire.

As he looked up, he realized Erin had shot ahead and was already at the mall entrance.

"Hurry up!" she called, then went inside.

Cursing, Kyle raced into the building. "Erin and the subject are in the structure, racing toward Twenty-first along the outside hall," he told Preston. "Move in and cut them off."

Erin was running down the tile walkway, and he had to weave in and out of the crowd to keep her in view.

Finally she stopped, turned in a circle, then looked back at him, clearly frustrated.

He caught up to her a second later. "Are you nuts? You could get yourself killed running after—"

Noticing a woman in her mid-twenties holding two toddlers by the hand and watching him closely, Kyle realized she'd seen the pistol at his belt.

"I'm a law enforcement officer, ma'am," he said quietly, pulling out his badge. "You're in no danger."

Erin gave the woman and her children a big smile. "Did you notice a man in a gray shirt, baseball cap and tan pants hurry by?"

The woman nodded. "He ran in there." She pointed to an all-night drugstore.

"Thanks, ma'am," Kyle answered. "Do you know if that place has a street side exit?"

"No, not for sure, but most of the stores here don't have one," she said.

Kyle looked past the woman at Preston, who was approaching at a brisk walk. Signaling his brother with a quick wave of his hand, he went with Erin into the large drugstore. "Stick close," he told her.

"I know what you're trying to do, but your plan would work better if we split up," she said.

"No. You're not armed," he snapped.

They checked the entire store, aisle by aisle, then with the manager's permission checked the back. There was a door there marked Emergency Exit.

"Maybe he's running back to his van," she said. By then Preston had joined them.

"I've got a security guard out front and a uniform over by the van now," he announced. "If the suspect goes back there, we've got him."

"I also punctured a tire. He won't be going anywhere quickly," Kyle said.

They hurried out to the parking lot, but the only person near the van was the uniformed officer.

"Did anyone fitting the description I sent you approach or pass by?" Preston asked him.

"No. I also double-checked the interior for stowaways but no one's there."

Kyle cursed. "We almost had him."

"Let's go through the van and see what we can get. I'm guessing it's stolen, but we may be able to lift some prints." Preston put on a pair of gloves, handed Kyle a second set, then opened the side door.

The two men climbed in, then Erin stepped closer to look inside. Several dark blue, flat plastic fibers in the carpeted area in the back caught her eye. They reminded her of the synthetic material used on sandbags or… "Guys, take a look at those fibers, and the white crystals scattered among them. The color and material match the ammonium nitrate bags Hank buys from Zia Limited."

Preston took a closer look. "I'll have the lab check this out ASAP."

"Did you say Zia Limited?" Kyle verified.

"Yeah, they're a solid company with plenty of experience handling explosives used by the mining and construction industries," Erin answered.

"That's where Frieda worked prior to getting a job at the bar," Kyle said.

"I'll check that out for you," Preston said.

"No. Hang back. It's better if they don't know we're onto them, at least until we find out what they've got targeted."

"So how do you want to deal with this? Have more feds come in?" Preston asked.

"No, that's the last thing I want. Get Daniel on this. I bet he deals with that company during training ops. See what he can get for us on Frieda."

"Yeah, that's a good idea," Preston answered. "Dan's friends with Clark Duncan, the owner."

"He can't let Clark know what he's doing," Kyle warned.

"No problem. I'll talk to him," Preston said. "Have you given any serious thought to where you'll hole up tonight?"

Kyle rubbed the back of his neck with one hand. "No, and I'm beat. We both are," he said. Erin nodded. "We need a secure place, but nothing obvious."

"I know the perfect spot."

"Can I go home to pick up a few of my things?" she asked.

"Not without the risk of being spotted," Kyle said.

"I can't keep wearing what I have on now," she protested.

"There'll be clothing at the safe house," Preston said. "Take whatever you need."

"How long will we be staying there?" she asked.

"One night, tops," Kyle said. "We have to keep moving." He saw her expression tighten. She wasn't pleased, but she'd accepted it, at least for now. He'd take that as a win.

"So where's the safe house?" Kyle asked his brother.

"I'll send the coordinates to your GPS," he said. "I'll also follow and make sure you're not tailed. On the way, I'll call Daniel and have him put two of his people on the job. If I take someone from the department, that'll leave a trail of its own."

"Good thinking," Kyle said. "Dan it is."

"Can I ask you a favor?" Erin said.

Kyle turned to look at her, but realized she was speaking to Preston.

"What do you need?" his brother asked.

"There's a potted plant on the windowsill next to my desk at the company office. Will you put it in a sunny spot, and water it for me?"

"You're worried about a *plant?*" Preston raised his eyebrows.

"It's a rare variety of desert rose, and I'd like to make sure it stays alive."

Preston looked at Kyle and saw him shrug. "Sure," Preston answered after a beat. "In fact, I'll take it to my office. I've got a sunny window there, and when this is over, you can pick it up."

"That would be great. Thank you, Preston. It may take it a decade to flower, but something tells me that when that spindly little thing finally blooms, it'll be well worth the wait."

"Some things are," Kyle said under his breath.

Once they got underway, Erin kept looking behind them.

"Stop doing that," Kyle said.

"I can't see your brother back there. Maybe you lost him," she said.

"He's there. Shaking off Preston would take a lot of fancy moves, and even then I'm not sure it could be done."

She lapsed into a lengthy silence, and he noticed she was grasping the handhold hard as he cut right, then left again on the route out of town.

"Aren't you ever afraid?" she asked.

"Sure, but I rely on my training and make it work for me. Fear keeps my senses sharp, and that burst of adrenalin gives me an added edge."

"Danger and you are old friends?"

From her tone, it was clear that she found the idea as appealing as sloshing through knee-deep mud. He smiled. "It suits me."

"Until something better comes along?"

Her question hit close to the mark, and it took him by surprise.

"I don't like to make long-term plans," he answered. "I've learned it's better to take things one day at a time. It saves me from disappointment."

The guarded look on her face made him realize he'd spoken too freely. He'd just admitted how well suited he was for the life of a hunter. Home, to him, would never be more than a temporary refuge between jobs.

Although it wasn't an earth-shattering admission, the fact remained that he'd lowered his guard, a luxury he couldn't afford if he planned on staying alive. That sweet face and body was a powerful distraction he needed to shut out.

A long silence stretched out between them, then as Kyle slowed to make a turn down a narrow graveled drive, Erin sat up.

"Oh, it's so pretty!" she said, looking ahead at the pale blue mobile home. "I love the picket fence, and the rose of Sharon around it."

Kyle parked, and as they got out, Preston, who'd pulled in just behind them, came over. "You'll have all the comforts of home," he said.

"I love it," she said and smiled.

He followed her gaze. "No, you're not staying in there, that's just the decoy."

"Then where…" She looked around, but there was nothing around for miles.

Preston pointed to the water tower about fifty feet away. "Just go up the ladder, then down the hatch."

"Wearing what, a bathing suit and a life preserver?"

Kyle smiled and nodded. "Expect the unexpected. I like it," he said, then took her hand. "Come on. Let's go."

Chapter Eight

As Erin descended the long, narrow steel ladder behind Preston, only a string of lights along the side of the ladder marked the way. Slowly her eyes adjusted to the gloom. For someone with a passion for sunlight and the outdoors, this didn't look promising.

She forced herself to push back the thought and keep going. The opening beneath them widened. Erin heard a muted click, and the area below them became illuminated in a soft light.

"It's beautiful," she said as they descended through an open hatch into a large, half-circle living area with two camel-colored couches, a bookcase filled with paperbacks, and beautiful wool throw rugs over what appeared to be tile flooring. In the other corner of the room was another open hatch, leading down to the next level. "Is it really safe in this water tower?"

"You're safer in here than you'd be anywhere else in the state above ground," Preston answered.

"The air you're breathing is drawn from secure, hidden inlets, then filtered. The water that comes out of the tap is drawn from the water table beneath this site, and the electricity comes through redundant lines, connected to a backup generator that can run for two weeks.

"There's also a communications/computer room in the third level equipped with monitoring equipment that'll give you a three-hundred-sixty-degree look at the area around you. Your satellite phone will work from here, too, Kyle, if you're on this level," Preston said. "Just keep it pressed against the wall. The outer shell serves as a giant antenna."

"The computers…encrypted?" Kyle asked.

"Absolutely," Preston answered, "like with that twenty-character code I entered in order to open the hatch. The only people who know the entry code are the governor, the mayor, and a designated department police officer, in this case, me. It would take years and a NSA mainframe to compromise the systems here."

"Paul told me about this place a year ago when he and I met in D.C. I thought he was pulling my leg."

"Nope. I've been told that every state has something along these lines, all placed away from the respective capitals. They're meant to serve as the governor's special refuge in case of extreme civil unrest or a terrorist attack. The parking lot outside is marked with infrared reflecting material for nighttime helicopter landings."

"It's like going through a high-tech version of *Alice in Wonderland*'s rabbit hole," Erin said, amazed.

"New Mexico chose a design that resembled an ordinary water storage tank, but it's far from that. The shell is impervious to anything less than armor-piercing ordnance. There are three levels and two exits—the way you came in or the emergency one, a subterranean tunnel on the bottom level that'll take you to the other side of the escarpment."

"The perfect safe house," Kyle said, looking at Preston. "Thanks."

"One last thing. You aren't here officially, so unless there's a statewide emergency, nobody'll find you."

"Okay, we're good then," Kyle answered.

"You won't really need Daniel's men in the area, but you'll have them and more. If anything's wrong, he'll make sure you get plenty of notice and backup," Preston said, then checked his watch. "It's late, so I'll leave you now so you can rest up."

After Preston left, they climbed down all the way to the bottom, exploring the various areas separated by partitions, then back to the middle level. The bedroom was there with a full-size bed and a huge armoire.

"Just one bed?" she asked. The prospect was undeniably exciting—but impossibly dangerous.

"The couch in the upper level turns into a bed, and I saw sleeping bags against the wall in the lower level where the computers are."

"So who'll take the bed? Shall we flip for it?" she asked, sitting on the edge of the bed and noting how comfortable it was.

"It's yours. Tonight I could sleep on the ground and never notice."

She sighed softly. "Yeah, I'm beat, too, but I'm not sleepy. After everything that's happened, I'm too wired."

"There are a lot of ways to relax," he said, giving her a slow, thoroughly masculine grin.

"I appreciate the thought but, no, thanks," she said, chuckling.

"Old-fashioned?"

"I wouldn't label it that. It's just that for me it's got to be more than just a chance to get hot and sweaty. If my heart's not in it, at the end all I'll feel is disappointed."

"I've never disappointed." He held her gaze.

Her skin prickled and her heart was pounding so hard she wondered if he'd hear it. "No matter how skilled, I need more than a man's hot body."

"I can respect that."

She paused. "Have you ever been married?"

"Me?" he asked, surprised. "No, no way. What

woman would want a guy who's gone nearly all the time, and whose work hours go under the category *till I'm done*."

Before she could answer, he walked to the armoire and opened it. "There's plenty of clothing here and on the shelves below. Take whatever you need. I'll grab a sleeping bag and stay by the computers and surveillance equipment. If you need me, that's where I'll be."

"Talk about changing the subject," she said with a tiny smile. "Let me see if I'm reading you right. You don't want to talk about anything personal, yet you're willing to have sex. You're a very strange man."

"Actually, I'm perfectly normal."

As he climbed down to the lower level for a sleeping bag, she sat on the edge of the bed and looked around. Her life had been ordinary till this morning. Now here she was with a man who should have come with a warning label.

Erin reached into her purse and brought out the tiny kaleidoscope her mother had given her before she'd passed away. As memories came flooding back, she smiled.

Her mother, an artist, had always followed her heart, no matter where it led her. George Barrett, Erin's dad, had been her opposite, a planner, a man who looked before he leaped.

In a rare mother–daughter moment, Erin had

once asked her mom why she'd fallen in love with him. Two pieces of a puzzle had to be different to fit perfectly into each other, Rita Barrett had said. That's why opposites were so often attracted to each other.

The problem was, she wasn't at all like her mom. She liked making plans and looking ahead. The way she was drawn to Kyle, a man she barely understood, disturbed her.

Hearing a knock on the hatch brought Erin out of her musings. "Come in."

Kyle climbed into the room, holding a sleeping bag under one arm. "Just passing through. I need to make a call and report in."

"Go ahead. Do whatever you have to," she said.

He looked at the brass tube she was holding. "What's that?"

"It's an old-fashioned kaleidoscope. It was a gift from my mother. I keep it to remind me that although change can be scary, it can also bring good."

"So you don't believe that change is necessarily bad. It's just something that makes you uneasy."

She nodded. "Experience has taught me that it can bring some hard lessons. I got married right out of high school, and when it ended less than a year later, I needed to earn my own living, but I had no skills. Eventually I took community-college courses and got myself back on track," she said. "That change took me to a better place, but the transition was a real make-it-or-break-it experience."

"So you avoid getting caught off guard by the unexpected by planning for as many contingencies as you can," he said. "I get it, but for whatever reason, that doesn't work for me. Every time I make plans, they result in a dead end. There are too many variables in my life that get in the way."

"The difference between us is that you have family you can count on in times of trouble. There's no one I can depend on except myself," she said.

"My brothers will always have my back. That's true," he said.

"Tell me more about them, or is that off-limits?"

He shook his head. "There are six of us. We all grew up in foster care, busy getting into trouble, until Hosteen Silver found us," he said. "Mr. Silver—*hosteen* is the Navajo equivalent of *mister*—was the kind of man who could scare you stupid with just one look. He never took any nonsense from any of us, but he was fair. Tough love, some might call it. Either way, he saw us as his sons and helped shape us into a real family."

"You were lucky life brought you together," she said.

"You're right about that. I'll tell you more about him someday, but for now I'd better get to work.

I've connected my cell phone to the surveillance system and we're fine outside. The cooler upstairs is empty, but we've got plenty of MREs and packaged energy bars. Here's one," he said, tossing it over.

"Thanks, right now I'm hungry enough to eat it—and the wrapper."

"We'll be leaving here at daybreak, so if you want, we can stop at Pancake Heaven on the way to Hartley."

"Daybreak? Why so soon? I thought you and your brother agreed this place was safe."

"No place is completely secure. Things have a way of going wrong when you lower your guard."

"Your job's taught you that the hard way, hasn't it?" she asked softly.

His expression hardened in the blink of an eye. "Let's just say I'm a good man to have beside you if you want to stay alive."

"What's it like to be a federal agent?" she asked, then added, "Not the IRS baloney—the guy who hunts down criminals and terrorists."

He smiled. "Would you be terribly disappointed if I were IRS?"

"Amazed would be more likely. I have difficulty believing an IRS agent who specializes in tax dodgers is so incredibly skilled at defusing bombs and shooting it out with killers," she said. "Since we're in this together, why not try a little honesty?"

He considered it, then at last nodded. "I'm an agent in the Naval Criminal Investigative Service. I'm involved because Hank Leland was working for the navy when he was seen associating with terrorists. Hank was also a naval reserve officer, which means we have jurisdiction in a case like this."

"Hank, working with terrorists? No way. Hank loved this country. There was no way he'd ever betray it."

"I believe you, and he did ask for our help earlier this morning," he said. "I went to find him right after I got word, but by then it was already too late."

"So now in addition to searching for his killers, you're looking for more detonators like the one you found in the box in Hank's office, right?"

"You saw what I took?" he asked, surprised.

"Yes. But why would Hank mail a detonator back—" She stopped and nodded. "They're hard to get here in the States without licenses and paperwork, but maybe not so much in Spain," she added, answering her own question.

"Exactly."

"Since it's not likely Hank mailed back just one, he must have hidden the rest somewhere. That's got to be what the men wanted when they came to the office. Now you have to find those detonators before they do."

"That's it in a nutshell. Good deductive reasoning. Now get some rest while you still have the chance," he said.

Kyle climbed up the ladder to the opening in the ceiling and closed the hatch behind him.

Erin took a deep breath, trying to stay calm. Kyle was unpredictable and dangerous, but those were great qualities for a bodyguard.

The problem was with her. Whenever she looked at him, she just couldn't keep her mind on business. Kyle was hot and edgy. He made her yearn for things she had no business wanting—a caress in the dark, the heat, the passion.

She'd prided herself in being strong, and had pushed back those longings for more than the feel of the hot New Mexico sun on her skin. Now the same strength that had fueled her pride whispered another truth. Sometimes a person's greatest loss lay in risks not taken.

IT WAS COMPLETELY dark in her room when the loud thump overhead woke her. The blackness was so encompassing it was frightening. At home, she usually left her bedroom curtains open a crack. She liked seeing the stars and the moonlight playing on the leaves of the cottonwood just outside her window.

Erin lay still, trying to figure out what she'd heard. It could have been Kyle moving around, or maybe some routine mechanical function. Several more minutes of silence went by. Finally, convinced it was nothing, she was about to doze off again when she heard a faint thump. In the stillness of their hiding place, two distinct and separate sounds were unnerving, and she had no idea where the second noise had come from.

She tossed the covers back, blinking and hoping her eyes would adjust quickly, but it remained pitch black to her. Fumbling for her purse, she found a penlight she kept in there for emergencies. She aimed the beam around the room, but no one was there, and both upper and lower hatches were closed.

She should go down and wake Kyle, then they could take a look around together. She thought about turning on the light, but if someone were roaming around in the facility, the glow might alert them.

Erin opened the hatch in the floor, then crept down the ladder. She could see without the penlight here, thanks to the computer screens and communications gear just beyond the partition. Kyle had said he'd be sleeping in the communications room, so he had to be around somewhere.

As she went toward the partition, a hand snaked around her from behind, and covered her mouth.

Surprised, she froze for a second, but recovered quickly and rammed her elbow into the person's gut. There was no reaction, not even a grunt.

"It's me. Why are you sneaking around? What's wrong?" Kyle whispered in her ear.

"I heard a thump upstairs," she answered when he uncovered her mouth. "Then I heard another one, coming from somewhere else. I thought someone had managed to break in."

He relaxed and released her completely. "Sorry. That was me. I went to the upper level to get a power bar and accidently let the hatch go as I was stepping up onto the floor. It thumped pretty loud. You didn't react, so when I came back down, I assumed I hadn't woken you up. Then when I heard the roof hatch open and footsteps on the ladder I thought we'd been compromised."

"I thought the same thing, and I didn't want to call out and give away my location," she said.

Even in the dim light, she was aware of everything about him. Kyle looked formidable shirtless and clad in low-slung jeans, pistol tucked into his waistband. His chest was muscular, his hips narrow. A dark line of hair ran down the center of his chest and stomach and disappeared into the regions below.

Her heart was stuck in her throat and her breathing unsteady.

"I'm really sorry I scared you," he said, lightly brushing his knuckles on her face and stepping closer.

His gaze held hers, and although she knew she should move away, she couldn't will herself to do so. Reflected in his gaze, she felt powerfully feminine and alive.

Slowly his mouth covered hers. At first, his kiss was gentle and she melted into him, loving his warmth and tenderness. She didn't want to think, she just wanted to *feel*.

As Kyle deepened their kiss, he became more insistent and demanding. She pressed herself against him and welcomed his roughness, seduced by that dark passion.

Soon she was lost in a river of fiery sensations. Pleasure rocked her as he moved his hand beneath her shirt, cupping her breast.

Everything in her wanted to surrender, to let nature guide them. She wanted more…of him.

The realization jolted her, and taking an unsteady breath, she stepped out of his arms. "No."

After an instant's hesitation, he released her.

"It's the darkness," she said, suddenly afraid of what she'd almost let happen. "It's too…easy to lose control."

"I'll turn on the lights," he said.

She watched him cross the small room. What

the heck was happening to her? This rush of emotions, of hormones… She hadn't felt like this since high school, and look how that had worked out. She'd ended up in an ill-fated marriage that had nearly broken her.

As a teenager she hadn't known any better, but now she did. She wouldn't let anything like this happen again.

As Kyle turned around, the lights now on, she could see he was back in control of himself.

"You should go back to your room. I'm going to stay up for a while. I want to check the monitors," he said, his tone cold and emotionless.

He walked with her to the hatch, climbed up and opened it for her. "You're safe, Erin," he said.

Then, as she climbed up the ladder, he added in a quiet voice, "Even from me."

It had barely been a whisper, but she'd heard him just as she closed the hatch. Her heart still racing, she brought out her penlight and found her way to the bed.

Sometimes the enemy that was hardest to fight was the one within yourself. Kyle Goodluck had saved her life, but now she'd have to safeguard her heart.

Chapter Nine

Kyle walked over to the sleeping bag spread out atop a foam pad. He slept far less often than anyone realized. Whenever he was working a case, he seldom went to bed before three or four in the morning. By then, exhaustion almost always guaranteed him some sleep. During slow times, he made it a point to work out hard. Otherwise, he'd end up staring at the ceiling for hours on end, nightmarish images, memories of a time and place he'd rather forget crowding his mind.

A little over a year ago, he'd been part of an operation that had made him question everything he believed about himself and his work. Knowing good men were needed to keep evil in check, he'd gone into law enforcement ready to meet the challenge, but he'd never realized the cost that battle would exact on him.

Hearing the muted vibration of his cell phone, he picked it up. It was not only encrypted, it would transmit a fake GPS signal that would prevent anyone from tracking him.

He looked at the screen, and seeing the name there, smiled. His brother Daniel was a workaholic and a night owl just like him. How he'd ever found a woman to put up with him remained a mystery. Yet these days Daniel seemed so settled, happy and undeniably at peace.

"Hey, bro, what's up?" Kyle asked.

"I figured you'd be awake," Dan said. "I spoke to Clark Duncan at Zia Limited, and he's given me full access to his inventory records. I'll get you an accounting of the explosives he's supposed to have on hand and you can check that list against what's actually in the warehouse. I'll have everything you need by tomorrow morning. Clark will be out with his men till late afternoon but he's instructed the guard at the gate to let you through."

"Thanks, that's great."

"After you're done there, come by my office. I'm helping HPD process some emails found on the Secure Construction server. Did Erin tell you that she'd emailed her boss once a day while he was overseas?"

"No, anything of interest in those emails?"

"Not so far, but I plan to process them for hidden ciphers."

"My gut tells me that's going to be a waste of time. Erin doesn't fit the profile of someone involved in terrorism."

"Which would make her the best kind of operative," Daniel said. "Don't lower your guard."

"We'll be on the move again in a few hours. I'll talk to you then."

He wasn't sure when he finally drifted off to sleep, but a muted sound close by jolted him awake. All his senses sharp, he sat up, gun in hand. Erin was standing a few feet away, her eyes wide open and the cup of coffee in her hand shaking badly.

He put the gun down immediately. "Sorry. Reflex action. Thanks for the brew," he said, taking it from her.

"It's instant, but I found a microwave, so the coffee's hot."

He glanced at his watch. It was seven. "You ready to go?"

"Yeah, next place we stay, can we try a safe house with stairs instead of ladders and access to a restaurant that specializes in green-chile cheeseburgers?"

"Sounds like you're starving," he said.

"We haven't eaten a real meal in almost twenty-four hours. Survival bars and candy don't count. I read some of the labels on the food they keep upstairs on those metal shelves and it sounded awful. I need real food. I don't know about you, but I enjoy eating. It helps me relax."

"So you need your chile fix?" he teased.

"You bet, and I know just the place. They have the most amazing milk shakes there, too. Since I've saved a gazillion calories lately, I can splurge."

He checked her up and down slowly. "You don't look like you have to watch your weight."

"That's because I watch what I eat. I'm also active and burn off calories working outside. Of course green-chile burgers are excellent for you— meat and vegetables all at once."

"You actually want a burger for breakfast?"

"Kyle, normal people eat three meals a day. We can have breakfast and later, lunch, too." Her smile brightened. "Hey, if you let me go by my house I could pick up some of my own chopped chile. It goes with just about anything. I guarantee you've never had anything like it before."

"Sorry, we still can't go to your place. It's too big a risk. If you need more clothing than what's available here, give me your size and what you need and I'll make sure you get it."

"I already took a clean change and a spare," she said. "I was just hoping…"

"I know," he said, and smiled. "When this is over, I'll take you up on that offer."

They were on their way less than ten minutes later. They never saw the men that had guarded them through the night, though as they left, the SUV that had been there when they arrived followed them to the highway.

"I'm glad we're leaving that place," she said. "It's like living in a missile silo."

"For an outdoorsy woman, you're not that big on roughing it," he teased.

"I've never gone backpacking in my life and have no desire to do so. My work outside is about growing food."

"My foster dad believed we should all learn to work with Mother Earth. A man who could hunt and grow food would always be able to feed his family," he said. "One year my brothers all competed to see who could grow the most ears of corn."

"How did that go?"

"Daniel drowned his plants. I went the opposite direction, trying to mimic the way the old pueblo people grew corn, planting the seeds deep in arroyos and low spots where water collected. Unfortunately, a lot of my plants never made it to the surface. Preston did everything with precision, hand watering each plant, and grew one heckuva garden," he added.

"Gene followed the advice of the *Farmers' Almanac* and his garden was better than Preston's. Rick and Paul decided to combine forces. One patrolled for weeds, the other watered. Their crop should have been the best, but wasn't. Gene won."

"Interesting," she said.

"Hosteen Silver said it was because Gene understood Mother Earth and worked with her instead of going to war." He laughed, remembering. "Considering Gene's got two toddlers a year apart, I'd say he understood nature a little too well," he added, giving her a playful wink.

"Is he happy with his family?" she asked.

"Oh, yeah. Out of all of us, Gene was the only one who was practically made to settle down."

"What about Daniel and Preston?"

"Preston got married a month ago. Daniel, about two years ago. They're both crazy about their wives and family."

"And the others?"

"You'll meet Paul sooner rather than later, I think. He owns a share in Daniel's company. He's married, too, and has adopted a four-year-old boy."

"What about your other brother?"

"Rick? He's single, like me, and out of the country now on assignment. I think we're the only confirmed bachelors, married to our jobs."

"Doesn't it get lonely working the kind of job you do, always traveling, but never staying anywhere for long?"

"I'm always too busy to think about stuff like that."

Yet, lately, during nights when sleep refused to come, he often found himself taking stock of his life. His work as an NCIS agent just wasn't a good fit for him anymore and he needed to find a new direction. Of course he'd always be an investigator. It was what he did best, and, fortunately, that left him with plenty of options.

THEY STOPPED FOR breakfast at a café along the highway, and after a breakfast burrito smothered in cheese and green chile, Erin felt better than she had since coming to work yesterday.

"I know Hank is gone, but it still doesn't seem real to me," she said, finishing her coffee and staring blankly out the window into the parking lot.

"Death is hard to accept. It's particularly difficult when someone you know well dies suddenly."

She nodded, lost in thought. "Hank was a good boss. He wasn't perfect, but I respected him and he, me. I'm assuming his brother will want to take care of the funeral arrangements once the body is released, but I really don't know."

"We'll be paying Joe Pacheco a visit this morning. Maybe he'll have heard something about that. Afterward, we'll go to Zia Limited," he said.

"Would you like me to call Joe on our way there just to make sure he'll be home?" she asked.

"No. I don't want to give him time to think about his answers. I need hard facts from him, not opinions based on the bits and pieces he's heard."

"Joe's home is the third house on the right," Erin said as they drove up the residential street. Four elementary school children with backpacks were standing on the sidewalk, talking, as they passed by.

"So you've been here before?"

"Not inside his home, no, but I dropped Joe off one afternoon when he couldn't get his pickup started," she said, as Kyle parked at the curb beside the house. "There's his oldest boy, Joe Junior, coming out now."

Joe came out onto the porch just then, looked over at the SUV, then ordered his son back inside.

"Dad, I'll miss the bus!" the boy protested.

"Don't worry about it, Junior. Your mother will take you to school. Now go inside."

The boy, curious, slowed to take a look at them, then hurried past his dad and went inside.

"I wondered how long it would take an officer to come by," he said, walking across the lawn and looking at Kyle, who'd exited the vehicle. Glancing at Erin, who was stepping down from the high profile SUV, he added, "But I didn't expect to see you."

"It's a long story," she answered.

Kyle flashed his badge, but Joe's laser-sharp gaze took in the details quickly. "Federal," he said, "but not FBI. Do you have a photo ID?"

"If you need further confirmation, go ahead and call the Hartley P.D.," Kyle said.

"Don't mind if I do," he said, stepping away. Joe had a cell phone in his hand, and quickly touched the screen, calling up a number. He spoke hurriedly to someone on the other end, waited several seconds, then apparently talked to someone else. After a short time he ended the call and walked over to join them.

"So the feds have taken over the homicide case, but it's not in the Bureau's hands. What's going on? Drugs? Smuggling? Something else?"

"We were hoping you'd have some of the answers, Joe," Erin said.

Joe gave her a long, hard look. "He's hauling you around?" he asked, not expecting an answer. "Is it protective custody, or is he using you as bait?" he added, then looked at Kyle.

Erin stared at Joe for a moment. His statement had been brutally blunt, more so than Joe normally was. Maybe he was trying to push Kyle's buttons.

Kyle didn't react, except with his eyes, which narrowed slightly.

"Maybe we should take this inside?" she suggested, trying to break the tension she felt building between the two men.

"Once my wife leaves with my son. I want to keep them out of this."

Kyle's gaze dropped. "You packing?"

"You bet," he said without hesitation. "I've got a concealed carry permit," Joe added. "There's something bad going on. I can smell it, and there's no way it's going to touch my family."

"What's sending you warning signs?" Kyle pressed.

"Several weeks ago there was an article in the local paper about Secure Construction and how it was one of the community's top-grossing companies. The reporter also mentioned that Hank had landed a big government contract building safe rooms at a U.S. naval base in Spain. Then, less than twenty-four hours after the boss returns home, someone tries to kidnap him and he gets killed. No way those things aren't connected."

Joe's observations were on target. With everything that had happened, Erin had forgotten all about that article. Everyone in town knew Hank's business.

A moment later, an SUV carrying a woman and a boy backed out onto the driveway. Once they'd disappeared around the corner of the residential street, Joe led Kyle and Erin inside.

"Actually, I'm glad to see you, Erin. I've been waiting to hear what's going to happen to our jobs," he said, taking them to the dining area, and picking up a mug of coffee off the table. "Should my men finish the on-site work we're doing now, or put everything on hold?"

"I'm not sure. I haven't had a chance to speak to Moe Jenner and ask him what's in Hank's will."

"I tried calling Moe earlier. He's on a fishing trip in the Gulf of California. Ron Mora, his paralegal, told me he doesn't know how to get hold of him. All he can do is leave voice mail and hope Moe comes ashore at a place with cell service."

"Moe always gives his paralegals a special code whenever he goes on vacation in case there's an emergency. He told me that himself," Erin replied.

"Why don't you talk to Ron then?" Joe said. "You're bound to get further with that little weasel than I did. I told him what happened and tried to convince him to track Moe down, but he said something like this could wait another week."

"Ron's new, and I think Moe intimidates the heck out of him. You, too, Joe," Erin answered. "Maybe it's the ex-cop in you. I'll give him a call, but not with you two listening to every word I say. It'll make me self-conscious, and Ron's bound to notice."

"Use the portable phone in the den," Joe said, waving her to the next room.

"Thanks," she said, and walked off.

As SOON AS she'd stepped out of the room, Joe's eyes locked with Kyle's. "Okay, what's going on, and why is an NCIS agent investigating a case in New Mexico?"

Chapter Ten

Kyle, though surprised, kept his poker face on. "I'm what?"

"Cut the bull," Joe said. "You flashed the badge like a magician working a card trick, but I know what I saw. I didn't want to blow whatever cover you cooked up, but I'd like to know what's really going on."

"Once a cop, always a cop, huh, Joe?" Kyle responded.

Joe pointed toward the coffeepot, and when Kyle shook his head, sat down at the table and waved Kyle to an empty chair. "Tell me what's going on. You cut a few corners with the local P.D. and scored some interagency cooperation, but Chief Sevilla wouldn't have given you that much latitude unless he'd been pressured by someone way above his pay grade. You think this is connected to how antsy Hank was acting yesterday morning?"

"Tell me about that," Kyle said.

"It was nothing overt. You'd have had to know the man to see it. He'd come in early, so I went to welcome him back and talk to him about our latest on-site job. Normally Hank will focus exclusively on what I have to say, but yesterday he was distracted and pumped up, like he'd had too much coffee. He told me to take a seat, then kept searching through a couple of cardboard boxes that contained pieces of tools and instruments some fool had taken apart. He was only half listening to me, and that was way out of character. After a minute, he put the box on the floor, out of the way, and I thought he was finally ready to talk, but he just kept looking around for something."

"Did you ask him what was going on?"

"Yeah, and I offered to help him find whatever he was looking for, but he shook his head." Joe rubbed the back of his neck with one hand. "Considering what's happened, I should have pressed him, but at the time, all I knew was that something was bugging him."

"Any idea what that might have been?"

"No, but if Hank was in trouble, I'm certain it had something to do with his brother. That guy's got a gambling problem. Hank bailed him out several times, then finally told him to man up, and deal with it. That, by the way, happened one day in the warehouse and we all heard. Everyone felt awkward, but the guy had it coming."

"Bruce still works for Hank, right?"

"Yeah, but not on a regular basis and never in a supervisory capacity."

Kyle stepped closer to the doorway leading into the room where Erin was speaking on the phone.

"Okay, now what's the deal with you and Erin?" Joe asked.

Kyle stared at him curiously.

"If she were really in protective custody she'd be stashed away someplace where no one would think of looking." When Kyle didn't answer, Joe's eyes narrowed. "Hank just spent weeks doing classified work at an overseas naval base. You think she's compromised his work, or maybe been stealing from the company?"

Kyle stayed close to the doorway, and met his gaze, but his expression revealed nothing.

"If you believe any of that, you're wrong about her," he said flatly.

"What makes you so sure, Joe?"

"I know Erin. I met her eight years back when I was still with the department. Her husband had been a local hero, the high school quarterback everyone thought would be playing college ball, and maybe even go pro someday. Instead, he got into drugs, painkillers at first, then went downhill from there. Eventually he OD'd and died in some downtown alley. By then she'd left him, but with nothing except a high school diploma and a father who was dying of cancer, life was real tough for Erin. She got back up on her feet, though. I met her again years later when I started working at Leland's. She'd already worked her way up to office manager."

They both looked over as Erin returned to the room.

"Ron told me he got through to Moe right after you called, Joe," she said. "Moe told him where to find a copy of Hank's will, and asked him to make it available to the police."

"Did he tell you what's in the will?" Joe asked.

"Yeah. Hank's will—actually, it's a trust—apparently stipulates that Secure Construction should stay open until all current jobs are completed. After that, the company is to be sold to the highest bidder. Whatever's left, once all the bills are paid, is to be divided among the employees. Hank and Moe set up a sliding scale based on how long each person has worked for the company."

"That answers my question. We have work to finish, and you can still cut payroll," Joe said, then as an afterthought, added, "I hope Mike Bewley's not going to be on that list of people who'll get a share of the proceeds."

"He's not a current employee, so I think we're safe on that score," she said.

"Who's Bewley?" Kyle asked immediately.

"He was one of our foremen—that is, until

Hank found out he was switching out construction materials with lower quality stuff and pocketing kickbacks. He got fired," Joe said.

"When did that happen?" Kyle asked.

"About three months ago, I think," Joe said, and looked at Erin for confirmation.

"Sounds about right," Erin answered.

"I heard that he's been having a tough time finding work. Seems word got around," Joe added.

"I'll look further into that," Kyle said. "Meanwhile, I'd like to get the Hartley P.D. to post an officer close to your house in case you run into trouble, Joe."

"No thanks. I'm going to send my family out of town to my sister-in-law's for a while. They'll be safe there. I'll stick around, of course, but I can look out for myself."

"You can't be awake all the time," Kyle warned.

"I've got all kinds of monitoring stuff here," he said. "I can also handle an intruder if I have to, and I know how to dial 911."

"All right. It's your choice. If you think of anything else that might help us wrap this all up, call me," Kyle said, handing Joe a card with his cell number and nothing else.

"Feds. You're all a veritable fountain of information, aren't you?" Joe muttered, studying the card.

"I'm one of the good guys," Kyle said, meeting his gaze. "That's what counts."

ONCE THEY WERE back in the SUV, Kyle called his brother and described their meeting with Joe.

"I hadn't heard about Bewley. I'll check him out for you," Preston said.

"I've also been working, and have what you need," a familiar voice piped in.

"I appreciate your help, Dan," Kyle said.

"No problem, little bro."

Daniel was two inches taller and never failed to rub it in. Kyle grinned.

"I've got that list of explosives and other related inventory Zia Limited has in storage. I'm sending it over to you right now."

"Just to verify, he's giving us run of the place?" Kyle asked.

"Yeah, and he trusts me, so leave everything the way you found it. Clark's compulsive about order. You'll see that when you visit his warehouse. If anything's missing, I'll guarantee it'll be easy to spot."

"Thanks for the heads-up. We're on our way there now."

"One more thing. I found out that one of Frieda's many clerical duties there was inventory control."

"Why did she leave?" Kyle asked.

"Clark fired her because she was sloppy with details—but, in this case, you've got to look at the source. By his standards, most people are. He has a high rate of turnover."

After getting directions to Zia from Dan and programming it into the GPS, they headed to the site, just outside Hartley's city limits.

"With the exception of your brothers, you don't trust anyone," Erin pointed out.

"Is there a question in there?" he asked, wondering where this was going.

"I don't like fighting on the same team with a man who doesn't trust *me*."

He glanced at her, then back at the road. "You heard Joe and I talking?"

"Not everything you said, but enough," she answered. "Here's what I don't get. Why are you protecting me if you think I may be out to harm you?"

"I don't know where you fit in, and until I have more facts, I can't afford to lower my guard," he said. "In my business that's what keeps a guy in one piece."

"But the way you kissed me…"

"You don't like my technique?" he said, eyes dancing.

"That's not my point," she answered. "If you're not sure of me, how could you—"

"Sometimes adding a little danger to the mix can spice things up."

She sighed loudly. "That's where we differ. Danger goes hand in hand with fear, and fear is the opposite of love."

He didn't answer, his attention on the rearview mirror, his expression hard.

"Are we okay?" she asked.

"Yeah, I'm just being careful," he replied.

Kyle Goodluck was big trouble. He brought an incredible single-minded intensity to everything he did—whether it was kissing her or hunting down a killer.

Her gaze slowly took in the way his strong hands gripped the wheel. Those big hands could be incredibly gentle, too....

"You have a little smile on your face. What are you thinking?"

"Nothing."

"Try again," he said with a ghost of a smile.

"You're good with women, and I'm sure you know how to get exactly what you want, but I'm not in your league. My lifestyle would bore you to death."

"We're different, that's true, but every man needs balance to walk in beauty. That's what Hosteen Silver taught us, and that man was always right."

"So what are you saying?"

"Yin and yang, black and white, day and night, both are needed to make things complete. Man and woman also become stronger when they balance each other out."

"What he taught became his gift to you. What a beautiful legacy," she said softly.

"I can appreciate it now, but at the beginning, it was a different story. I was convinced that spiritual stuff was what adults used to control others. Hosteen Silver knew how I felt, too, and never pushed anything on me. He figured actions spoke louder than words, and I'd come around eventually."

"And you did."

He nodded. "As time went by, I began to see the value of what he was teaching us. He lived in tune with everything around him, at one with the pattern. Everything about him spoke of what we call *'áli̇ l,* power not easily seen by the material senses."

"I think everyone, to one extent or another, wishes they could meet a man like Hosteen Silver."

"Living with him wasn't always easy," he said, "but the man helped us see ourselves in a new light. Without him, I'm pretty sure I would have landed in jail. I was always looking for trouble, testing myself, pushing the limits."

"You still are."

He chuckled. "Maybe, but now my actions have purpose. What I do is for the greater good."

"See that? You and I aren't so different after all."

"You've lost me," he said.

"On the face of it, it appears we're worlds apart, but we're not. You're in law enforcement and I'm a farmer, but our goals are the same—make life better for others."

His eyebrows rose. "That's one way of looking at it."

Kyle signaled, slowed, then made a right turn off the main road onto an industrial side street lined with one-story metal warehouses. Three buildings down, he turned up an alley, then made another left, pulling to a stop behind a used-RV sales lot.

"What's going on? Your GPS keeps recalculating 'cause you're making it crazy. If you don't want to use it, shut it off," she said.

He sat back, his eyes on the intersection they'd just passed. "I think we're being followed. I saw a silver-gray sedan when we left Joe's. Then it disappeared. A few minutes ago, I saw the same car again. If it's really tailing us, it'll pass by us in another minute—like right now."

Chapter Eleven

Kyle pointed to the silver car that cruised by slowly. "He's searching for us. Time to put ourselves in *his* rearview mirror for a change."

Kyle drove to the corner, then pulled out several car lengths behind the sedan. It had New Mexico plates, and there was only one person inside, the driver.

"You're right," Erin whispered. "He's looking around, trying to figure out where we went."

Their tail drove up to the next intersection, came to a stop at the sign and looked left and right.

Kyle stopped in his lane, waiting, still several car lengths behind the sedan.

"Shouldn't we get—?" Erin began, when the sedan suddenly roared to life and raced through the intersection. An oncoming pickup was forced to hit the brakes to avoid T-boning it.

Kyle leaned on the horn as he raced past the intersection, whipping around the pickup, and accelerating after the fleeing sedan. "Hang on!"

They entered a street that led past a big auto-repair warehouse. Vehicles lined both sides of the road, which narrowed up ahead to barely two lanes. The sedan took the center, but didn't have the horsepower Kyle's SUV did and they closed the gap rapidly.

The sedan's brake lights came on suddenly as the driver swerved right, then abruptly cut left. This time he nearly collided with an oncoming truck and trailer stacked with brand-new cars.

Kyle knew he'd never make the turn, so he accelerated past the truck driver, whose attention was probably focused on saving his own load.

"Maybe we can cut off the sedan up ahead," Kyle said, glancing over at the GPS road map.

Ignoring the next stop sign, Kyle raced through the intersection and made a hard left, turning up a road that ran parallel to the one the sedan had taken. "He'll have to head in this direction eventually. The street he took is a dead end."

Erin nodded, also watching the GPS screen. "But if he circles back before then, we've lost him."

"I know."

"In his shoes, what would you do?"

"I'd circle back," he said, then added, "Okay, then. I'll take the next left and try to intercept him." Kyle slowed as they drove down the intermediate street.

"I'll watch my side," Erin said.

After a few minutes, they reached the street the sedan had originally taken, and were forced to circle, checking every vehicle they passed.

Ten minutes later, Kyle cursed. "Lost him. Might as well go over to the warehouse. At least he never found out where we were headed."

"And if he did, we'll come across him again, right?"

"Yes, but that won't be the case. In my opinion, he's long gone."

"Do you think he was watching Joe's place and decided to follow us instead?"

"No, I checked the parked cars near his home and no one was keeping watch. Unless they used special long-range surveillance equipment, but that's not likely."

"So how do you account for what happened?"

"The way I see it, they figured out where we were *after* we arrived at Joe's. Maybe someone was on foot watching the house, and I missed him."

She waited a while before speaking again. "The people you're looking for are trained and persistent. That's a bad combination. And you think I'm somehow connected with these people?"

"Okay. How did you get to be so handy with a pistol?"

"Dad didn't get a son, he got me. So I learned

to fish, work on cars, drive a tractor, and I was also taught to shoot and safely handle a gun. Good thing, huh?"

"Sounds like you two were close."

"We were. My dad was a good man who worked hard to make his dream come true, but he ran out of time. After he got sick he had to sell the acreage he had along the river. It was prime farmland, where he'd planned to grow his special *Encanto* chile. *Encanto* means a sense of wonder and that's the way he wanted people to feel when they ate his chile," she said, then in a heavy voice added, "The end of his dream became the beginning of mine."

"What do you mean?"

"I swore I'd finish what he'd started."

"Do you regret that?" he asked.

"No, not at all. The land draws me just as it did him." She stopped speaking and looked at him. "I'm sorry. I've been going on and on, but I wanted to get what I've been feeling out in the open."

"Not a problem. I'm glad I'm finally getting the chance to know you better."

"So you can decide if I'm friend or foe?"

"Okay, there's that," he said, not bothering to deny it, "but I also admire your reverence for the land and the Plant People."

"The…Plant People? Farmers, you mean?"

"No, it's a Navajo thing going all the way back

to our creation stories. Our traditionalists see all plants as people who go where they will. They can also bless or harm, depending on how you appeal to them."

"That's right on target, particularly in the case of chile," she said. "Ever had it burn the roof of your mouth? That's a perfect example of a plant with attitude."

He laughed. "I like you, Erin Barrett."

"You may not trust me, but I make you laugh. Is that it?"

He laughed again. "Blunt and to the point. Good thing your dream didn't involve working in the diplomatic corps."

"People spend way too much time playing games and saying stuff they don't mean instead of calling things the way they are."

"You're right about that," he said, slowing down as they reached a gated, fenced-in compound.

As Kyle pulled up next to the guard's shack, the Navajo man there recognized him and immediately smiled. "Hey, dude, how you been? Haven't seen you since high school! I hear you're a federal cop these days," he said, peering into the car.

"That's right, Justin. Do you want to see my ID?"

"Nah. Daniel called my boss and Clark told me to give you run of the warehouse. If there's anything you need, just let me know," he said, and handed him a set of keys. "Building C, second to the left. Just you and the lady, right?"

"Yeah, and we might be a while."

"No problem. Just make sure you lock up and return the keys," he said, waving them through.

After entering the compound, Kyle drove straight in, passing buildings A and B, on the left and right, before Erin pointed out the warehouse. It was a hundred yards farther away and constructed of sheet steel. A big water valve, painted red, was located at one end of the building, which had a loading dock and concrete parking barriers.

"Kind of small," he commented, pulling into a parking slot, then bringing out his phone. "I was expecting something more like a big hangar."

"It fits the company's needs and it's protected from fire, weather and burglars," she said.

"You've been here before?" he asked.

"Once, a long time ago. It was part of my orientation. Hank wanted me to be familiar with every aspect of our business, so Clark gave me the guided tour."

Inside, the warehouse felt cool; the air flow from overhead fans kept the temperature steady. The scent of chemicals was faint, much less than he'd expected.

As they walked from labeled section to section, they passed pallets of bagged chemicals stored in a basket weave pattern that maximized space. In the four corners of the room were metal storage containers, like those carried on railroad cars or container ships, each holding different types of high and low explosives with appropriate red diamond warning labels.

"I didn't expect to see this much inventory in here," Kyle said, looking around. "Let's start by checking out the pallets of ammonium nitrate. Mix that with any number of other easily obtainable substances and you've got one of the cheapest, most available explosives in the world."

After noting the layout and location of those three pallets, he counted the rows that held the fifty-pound dark blue plastic bags. "Ten high, and five bags in each level, three wide, two long, perfect squares. That's a hundred and fifty bags total. It matches inventory," he said, walking around to examine the sides of the stacks, "but I can't see them from all four sides since they're against the wall, and that's a problem for me."

"I remember a local hay farmer who ran into trouble when he got caught shorting his customers by stacking the bales a certain way. Is that what you're thinking?" Erin asked.

"Yeah, and, stepping back, I think that center stack looks a little...skinny."

"Only one way to find out."

"Yeah, climb up and move around some bags,"

Kyle replied, "and that's exactly what I'm going to do."

"Can I help?"

"Can you handle that much weight?"

"I've stacked bags of sand and mortar before, as well as fifty- to sixty-five-pound bales of alfalfa. Just don't rush me, okay?"

Ten minutes later, after moving aside three layers of bags, they discovered that the inventory was short. Kyle called Preston. "I've got two bags missing, and combined with the right chemicals that's a lot of explosive power. Did you get anything useful from the detonator I found in Leland's office?"

"Daniel's still working on that. I'm at his place right now, so why don't you come over?"

"I'll be there in twenty," he said. "Anything on Frieda Martinez yet?"

"We have a BOLO out on her, but we already know she cut her hair, and by now she's probably a brunette."

"Good point, but remember what Erin mentioned about Frieda's broken nose. That can cinch an ID."

After he hung up, he glanced at Erin. "Tell me more about Frieda."

"She was always upbeat around Hank and that never failed to improve his mood, but to me, it felt contrived—calculated. I looked deep into those feelings of mine, wondering if I was somehow jealous, but that wasn't it. Her smile never reached her eyes, do you know what I mean? I got the feeling she was who she was by design, like someone playing a role."

"Did you ever tell Hank how you felt?"

"No, it wasn't my place. Hank was my boss. His private life—and mine—were off-limits."

"His idea, or yours?"

She looked at him sharply, then relaxed. He hadn't been baiting her. "I set those ground rules from day one, not just with Hank, but with all the employees. I didn't want any complications or misunderstandings. That job was all I had."

"Tell me something, just how close are you to buying back your father's old field?"

"Taking raises into account, I figured that in another four years I'd have enough for a down payment on the land. Then, if I continued to watch my expenses, I'd hoped to be able to open Encanto Enterprises another four years after that."

"Setting a long-term goal like that, and seeing it through, usually carries a price, more than just money."

"I know. I've given up a lot of things I need just to stay on track. No one ever said it would be easy."

Soon they were back on the road headed to Daniel's place.

"My brother's office is totally secure," Kyle

said. "He and his wife even lived there for a while after they got married."

"But not now?"

"He was happy, but Holly wanted their home to be completely separate from business. Dan offered to build her a house on-site, but she didn't go for it."

He kept his eye on the rearview mirror, and made several evasive turns.

"Are we being followed?" she asked, glancing back.

"No. I'm making sure we aren't."

Erin remained silent a while. "The guys who killed Hank think I have the detonators and I understand why. Hank trusted me and instinct tells me that I *should* know where they are, but I don't." She expelled her breath in a hiss. "I've been trying to put myself in Hank's head and figure out where he hid them but I'm getting nowhere."

"Sometimes we beat things to death when what we need to do is let the idea come naturally. We'll be at Dan's soon. You'll meet Paul there, too. Relax, and get to know my family. Maybe a little downtime is just what you need."

"What if they're watching Daniel's place?"

He laughed. "If they try anything there, they'll have more to worry about than we will. Guaranteed."

Chapter Twelve

The fenced compound had an electronic gate and cameras mounted on tall posts. Yet as Kyle pulled up in his SUV, the gate automatically opened.

"Well, that's not very secure," she said.

Kyle laughed. "He has heat sensors and several other hidden gadgets monitoring the area. As soon as we turned up the access road, he knew exactly who we were. If we'd tried to crash the gate an electromagnetic pulse would have disabled the car. After that, we would have been outgunned."

"But no one's around," she said, surprised.

"Trust me. Dan's firm is on the leading edge when it comes to security."

As they approached the main building, two tough-looking Navajo men came out and stood by the door.

"The guy in black jeans and windbreaker, that's Daniel. The one wearing slacks and a tie is Paul. He must have met with a client today. Come on in."

Once inside, she noticed that the heavy steel door locked with a deep thud, like a bank vault.

Kyle introduced her, then followed his brothers to the office's computer center. A huge, horizontal computer screen the size and configuration of a table rested adjacent to four large monitors next to each other on the wall.

Daniel tapped several keys, and a photo of the detonator they'd found on Hank's desk came up on the table monitor. With a sweep of his fingertip he sent the image to one of the wall monitors. "I don't know who you're dealing with, Kyle, but this is serious stuff. The device is sophisticated, capable of being detonated by a remote signal even when security agencies are jamming cell-phone transmissions. These detonators are only available to special units of the Spanish military—the equivalent of our special forces, and were probably stolen. I'm trying to find out if Interpol has the serial numbers listed, and names of any suspects, but so far, no luck. These devices aren't state-of-the-art, but close to it."

"Can you forward your findings to my D.C. office?" Kyle asked him.

"Yeah, this terminal is secure. Do you want to encrypt it anyway?" Dan asked.

Kyle nodded. "Send it directly to Supervisory Agent Martin Hamilton. Here's the email address. He'll pick it up within seconds."

True to what he'd predicted, Kyle's satellite phone rang shortly thereafter. The transmission kept breaking up, so Kyle returned the call using one of Daniel's phones rather than having to step outside for a clear sight line.

"Yes, the connection's secure," Kyle assured him a moment later.

Daniel led Paul and Erin into the kitchen. "Let's give him some privacy," he said.

"All those rules and regulations are going to strangle him," Paul grumbled. "Kyle should come work for us."

"He will," Daniel said, "when he's ready." He looked at Erin and smiled. "This must seem like an alien world to you."

"No, more like a man cave with too many remotes," she answered. "I understand you lived here for a while?"

Daniel chuckled. "I found it homey, but my wife, not so much."

Paul poured her a cup of coffee. "Sugar?"

"No, plain's fine," she said, and took it from his hands.

"There was an article a few weeks ago in our local newspaper about the overseas contract Hank Leland had landed with the DOD, building safe rooms at a naval base. It told everyone where Hank Leland was and what he would be doing. I'm assuming he gave the reporter that information, or at least confirmed it. Why the publicity?" Paul asked.

"Hank had been wanting to expand, but he knew he'd need the name recognition to bring in more contracts and revenue."

"So what happens to the company now?" Paul asked.

She told him what she'd heard from Ron, Moe Jenner's paralegal.

"Wait—Moe Jenner is Leland's attorney?" Daniel asked her.

"Yeah, is something wrong?"

Just then Kyle walked in, and, glancing at their faces, added, "What's going on?"

"Not sure yet," Daniel said. "Let's go back into the computer room. I've got something I want to check out."

Daniel entered something into his computer, then looked up. "I was right. Since I saw the detonator, I've been keeping tabs on calls coming from the Hartley P.D. Earlier this morning Mrs. Jenner filed a missing person's report on her ex— Moe Jenner."

"Preston never said a word to me about it," Kyle said.

"He may not have heard. Moe was supposed to meet his ex and give her a check for the balance of the mortgage on their house, but Moe never showed. She called his cell and home, but both kept going to voice mail. She also called his office and, again, got answering machines," Daniel said. "The officers tracked down Ron Mora, Jenner's paralegal, and were told that Moe left town just to make the divorcée wait an extra week. Ron had supposedly been out of the office on personal business, and hadn't had a chance to return any calls."

"So basically the police don't consider him missing," Kyle said.

"Ron may be right about the delay. There was a lot of bad blood between Moe and his wife," Erin said.

"How do you know this?" Paul asked.

"Moe drops by the office every once in a while, and he and Hank share a drink. Although Hank's office door is always shut, I still hear things." Just then, they heard the door open and an attractive brunette walked in carrying two large paper sacks with a restaurant's logo. The food smelled heavenly and made Erin's mouth water. "Unless I miss my guess, you've got stuffed sopaipillas in there."

"Hey, Holly," Dan said, and went to give his wife a kiss.

"I brought lunch for everyone," Holly said. Glancing at Erin, she smiled. "I'm guessing all you've been eating is fast food—that's when you can get Kyle to actually stop long enough to pick up something."

"Yeah, that's about it," Erin answered with a wry smile.

"When Daniel called and said you two were on your way over, I decided to pick up some stuffed sopaipillas at Cuatro Hombres." Holly brought out paper plates and handed over three sopaipillas, then glanced at Erin. "Come on, girl. The guys are comfortable eating and working in here, but you and I can remain civilized and eat our meal in the kitchen on real dishes."

"Do you all need me here?" Erin asked.

"No, go ahead," Kyle answered. "My brothers and I need to brainstorm."

"Okay then." She looked at Holly and smiled. "Lead the way."

"I think comfort food is a necessity when things are tough, don't you? Warm, stuffed sopaipillas are the equivalent of a hug—and they taste better," Holly said, grinning.

"So tell me, what kind of chile do they use on these?" Erin asked, and out of the corner of her eye, saw Kyle smile.

ONCE IN THE KITCHEN, Holly reached into the cabinet and brought out some terra-cotta-yellow and Prussian-blue stoneware plates. "These dishes are gorgeous! I love the pattern and the bold colors," Erin said.

"Me, too."

The sound of loud voices echoed through from the next room, and Holly smiled. "That's how they crack tough cases. They bounce ideas off each other, argue and work things out."

"You know what's going on?" Erin asked.

Holly shook her head. "No, it's better if I stay out of things like this. Daniel has a way of getting completely wrapped up in his work, so I force him to keep our personal life and his business separate."

"I heard that he wanted to live here after your marriage, but you had other plans."

"Yeah, and now he sees I was right. The baby will grow up fast and Daniel wouldn't want milk and fruit juice all over the computers," she said, grinning. "The baby's at the sitter's today, so I get some hours off to run errands and relax."

Erin took a bite of the puffy stuffed sopaipilla and smiled. "Wow, this is great! Everything is so fresh and flavorful."

"I know the men who run the restaurant, and there's nothing those guys can't fix, but this is hands-down the best," Holly took a big bite and smiled happily. "Heaven. One of these days, I'm going to get their recipe."

"Do you like to cook?"

"You bet. I never did much of it when I was single, but when I know Daniel's going to be home, I like fixing traditional New Mexican meals. It's fun."

"You sound like a woman who loves her life," Erin said wistfully.

"I do, but when I first met Daniel, things were a lot different. I was in some really bad trouble and scared to death." She met Erin's gaze. "It's like that for you, isn't it?"

"Yeah, it is." Erin scooped a forkful of green chile and pinto beans into her mouth and grinned. "But this meal makes everything better."

"You need to trust Kyle. He and his brothers are as different as night and day, but they have one thing in common. They're solid as rocks, hard on their enemies, and completely loyal to a friend."

"I want to, but it's difficult because he doesn't really trust me."

"Well, I'm afraid that's something else they all have in common. Their backgrounds make it hard for them to lower their guard," she said. "But when it finally happens, you'll see it was worth the wait."

"I just wish…"

Holly smiled. "Kyle's getting under your skin, isn't he?"

Erin started to deny it, then stopped. "Maybe, but Kyle and I aren't a good fit. I love the land and setting down roots. He thrives on action and danger. A farmer can't give him that kind of rush."

"You'd be surprised," Holly said with a mysterious smile. "Hosteen Silver's men have a way of making what seems impossible, possible. Don't give up on him, not yet."

"THEY'RE HERE FOR a reason," Paul said. "They used Hank Leland, forcing him, somehow, to mail that box back to the U.S. What we have to find out is how many detonators they packed, and what he did with them before he was killed. These people came after him in broad daylight. Why risk exposing themselves like that unless what they have planned is really big?"

"That's what I'm thinking, too," Kyle responded, "I've got to find out where the rest of those detonators are, and get them before they do."

"I've compiled a list of potential targets for you," Paul said, and pointed to his computer screen.

Daniel and Kyle came to look over his shoulder. "The top three aren't going to give them the kind of publicity they want," Daniel quickly concluded.

"Number four looks like a big deal," Kyle said. "I've been out of the country for a couple of years, so I'm not up on tribal affairs. But what does a uranium mining company from Spain have to do with the dedication of a new tribal water pipeline?"

"A large percentage of the water delivered by this pipeline system is going to be used in a big test for an underground uranium extraction process. The water and other chemicals will be used to leach out uranium," Daniel explained.

"And the Spanish company is hoping to learn from this so they can enhance their own uranium extraction capabilities," Paul added.

Kyle thought about it a moment. "Daniel, do a search for groups in Spain protesting uranium mining and nuclear power plants. While I was over there, I recall hearing about attacks on those types of operations. Mining equipment was being blown up and company officials murdered."

Daniel quickly found the name of three suspected groups carrying out attacks on the Spanish nuclear-power industry.

He looked over at Kyle. "These people are motivated and ruthless. Unfortunately, based on reports from Spanish law-enforcement agencies and Interpol, no suspects have ever been positively identified. There are descriptions, and grainy photographs, but nothing more."

"I need to send them the photos of the dead perps. Maybe these will help establish some connections with individuals over there. We need to know if we're dealing with some of the same people."

"I'll send an email to Preston and his boss right now," Daniel replied.

"And to my supervisor, via Preston. Sign my name," Kyle added.

"This is our best lead yet," Kyle said. "From what I'm seeing on the screen, the dedication ceremony for the tribal water resource project provides bigger targets than these Spanish businessmen. It doesn't specify, but I have a feeling you already know who's on the guest list," he added, looking at Daniel.

"Yeah, my firm's handling part of the security, but all I can tell you is that we're expecting some big guns from the Washington, D.C. area. They're high-priority targets, by anyone's standards."

"We've all got clearance here, so don't hold back," Kyle insisted.

"These people are way above your pay grade, bro," Daniel said. "Cabinet members, and maybe more."

"Will it make headlines?" Kyle asked, refusing to back off.

"Oh, yeah," Daniel said.

"What's the date for that dedication?" Kyle pressed.

"It's in three days. The guest list won't be announced until the last minute because of political bickering back in Washington."

"Now I'm beginning to understand why my boss was willing to blow my mission by sending more agents down," Kyle said.

"This is heavy-duty stuff," Paul said. "You have

to stay sharp even though hanging out with Erin's going to distract you. That woman's *hot*."

"Watch your mouth," Kyle growled, then the instant he saw Paul smile, knew he'd been had.

"I'm right, aren't I? You like her. That means you're not thinking with your head, you're thinking with your—" Paul stopped short as Holly walked into the room.

"What? Did I disturb guy talk, or is this secret spy talk?" she asked with a tiny smile.

Daniel walked over and kissed her gently. "What do you need, sweetheart?"

"We had a small accident cleaning up in the kitchen and Erin needs a change of clothes. I've got some shirts and jeans here so I thought we'd go to the back room so she could try them out. Will you need her for something right away?"

"No. We'll be here for a while longer," Kyle said. "And thanks, Holly. I'll make sure you're reimbursed later."

"No need. I just wanted you all to know where we were going to be," Holly said.

After she walked out, Daniel glanced at Kyle. "You could use a change of clothes, too, dude. You wash that shirt in hot water? It must have shrunk two sizes."

"It's not mine. It was all I could get at Preston's safe house."

"I think we still wear the same shirt size, so take

what you need out of the closet down the hall before you leave," Daniel said.

Paul cleared his throat. "If you ladies are through discussing fashion, there's something I'd like to show you." He pointed to the screen as his brothers came over to join him. "Decryption software didn't turn up any hidden messages between Erin Barrett and the deceased."

"No surprise there," Kyle said. "Can you run a comprehensive background check on Bruce Leland for me? He's the vic's brother. Also, see what you can get on Mike Bewley. He worked for Hank, but was fired before Leland went to Spain. And if you get a photo of the man, pass it along to Daniel so he can add it to those images going to Spain and Interpol."

"Will do. Full background checks take time, but you've got less than three days, so give me some room, and let me see what I can do," Paul said.

ERIN ZIPPED UP the jeans she'd borrowed from Holly without having to take in a breath. "These fit just right."

Holly smiled wistfully. "After the baby, those are still too tight for me, so you're welcome to them." Hearing a dull thump, Holly winced. "Uh-oh."

"What's wrong?"

"The guys are in the gym, sparring or wrestling. They love to compete and test themselves whenever they get the chance. They're just messing with each other, but I've yet to figure out why they enjoy that so much."

"Sparring? You mean a fist fight?" she asked, her voice rising slightly.

"No. We wives insisted they use padded boxing gloves and put mats on the floor," Holly said. "They said we were taking away all the fun, but we refused to yield."

"But why fight each other now? We're in the middle of a battle."

"It's not really like that," Holly said. "I bet Daniel and Kyle were looking for a way to unwind, especially Kyle."

"Not Paul?"

Holly shook her head. "When he was a Federal Marshal he got shot, and there was a lot of damage. He doesn't say much about it, but I only saw him spar once, and that was with Daniel."

They heard boisterous laughing, then a curse.

"You want to go see?" Holly asked, smiling. "I never get tired of seeing my hubby without his shirt on."

"Kyle…too?"

"Yep, they strip to the waist."

"Then what are we waiting for?" Erin said, following Holly down the hall.

Erin couldn't take her gaze off Kyle. He was

quick as lighting, dodging his brother's jabs and matching him blow by blow. It wasn't much of a fight, really. They knew each other's best moves and most of their punches were blocked or dodged.

Erin watched Kyle's muscles tighten and flex. She would have given anything to run her hands over him and snuggle into that beautiful, bronzed chest.

"They do this for fun, can you believe it? I don't get it, but it's sure nice to watch," Holly said.

"Yeah, it is," Erin admitted, letting her imagination run free.

Finally Paul came over to the ropes and called out. "Guys, give it a rest. It's time to get back to work."

They broke up instantly, fist bumping with their boxing gloves before taking them off. Erin saw Kyle reach toward the chair that held his shirt and pick up a leather cord with a small pouch attached to it. He slipped it around his neck just as Daniel, standing about four feet away, did the same.

"What's in those leather bags?" Erin asked Holly quietly.

"All the brothers carry their own medicine pouches. They're gifts they received from Hosteen Silver," she said. "There's a lot more to it than that, but Kyle will have to tell you the rest."

Erin watched as the men shrugged into their

shirts and hurried back to the computer room. Curious as to what Paul had found, she followed.

As she entered the room, Erin heard Paul mention a six-figure sum of money. "That's what he owed them, but he managed to pay most of it back by selling off his car and house."

"Who?" she asked.

"Bruce Leland," Paul answered.

Holly appeared a moment later with Preston. "Here's everyone, Preston," she said, then smiled at the others. "I've got to get going, guys." Looking at Erin, she added, "You're in good hands."

"Just in time, bro," Kyle said. "Get the emails?"

"Yeah. Everything we have ID-wise is on the way to Spain and Interpol HQ," Preston replied. "What've you got?"

He took a quick look at the computer screen. "Bruce, huh? That's some gambling debt," he said. "I found out that Bruce also has a record for passing bad checks. He barely managed to stay out of jail."

"Hank knew about his brother's gambling habit and didn't trust him," Erin said.

"So what else have you found out since that last email?" Preston asked.

Paul filled him in on their theory concerning the water pipeline dedication. "Sounds like you might have nailed their motive and target, but three days isn't a lot of time," Preston said. "What's the plan?"

"We all work on this exclusively for the next forty-eight hours. If we don't get anything substantial, we have two choices. Cancel the event, which means the remaining terrorists will disappear into thin air, or let it go on as scheduled, and bring more agents down. If we do that, we run the same risk," Kyle said. "Bottom line—it's up to us to get results."

"We're in this with you all the way," Preston said.

Kyle saw Daniel nod.

"Time to get down and dirty," Kyle said. "Let's make some waves and see what surfaces."

As Kyle's phone rang, he glanced down at the screen. "It's Joe Pacheco," he said, answering it.

"I'm calling from my vehicle. I'm in a dangerous situation and I can use some backup," Joe said, his tone all business.

Chapter Thirteen

"I'm with law enforcement now, so I'm going to put you on speaker," Kyle said. "Tell me what's going on."

"I sent my family away in our RV, and just to make sure they left town okay, I decided to follow them for a while," Joe said. "That's when I spotted a dark blue van keeping pace with them. I came up behind it, then passed, letting the driver see me at the wheel. When I turned off, the van followed me instead of my family. It looks like I'm the target, not them."

"The van's still following you?" Kyle asked.

"Yeah," Joe answered, giving them his current location.

"So let's put the squeeze on them," Preston said, reaching for his car keys.

"Got that, Joe?" Kyle added.

"Copy. They follow me, and you find a way to trap the van between us. I'm in," Joe replied.

"Okay, keep moving and work your way toward

the west side of town if you can. Try to stay on streets with enough traffic so they can't risk forcing you over," Kyle said, gesturing to Erin to follow him as he brought out his SUV keys. Daniel and Preston were already heading toward the door.

"Once we're en route, update me on your location and we'll set up a pattern so we can close in," Kyle said.

Three minutes later, connected via phones or radio, they were headed east toward the city, which was only a few miles away. Joe was trying to buy time by making sure he caught all the traffic lights.

"Where you at now, Joe?" Kyle said as they reached the business area of Main Street. Beside him, Erin tracked their movements on the GPS display. Although both of them were familiar with the city's layout, he'd been gone for months. She was more likely to know of any recent road work or changes in traffic patterns.

Joe's voice was louder than normal, but to Kyle, it sounded more like the result of a rush of adrenalin rather than fear. "I'm going west past Orchard, but if I go much farther, it intersects with Melrose, and there'll be no side roads for your people to close in."

"He could take a left onto Fourteenth Street," Erin suggested, pointing to the map on the screen.

"Good idea," Kyle said. "Go with it, Joe, and

stay in the left-hand lane, like you're looking for a particular street," Kyle said. "Copy?"

"Copy that," Joe replied.

"Preston, Daniel, you copy?" Kyle snapped.

"Copy," Preston responded crisply. "I can approach from Hilton, reach Fourteenth ahead of Joe, then take the lead."

Daniel joined in. "I'm only a block behind Preston. "I'll wait until Joe's vehicle passes, and cut in between him and the van. Hopefully, the van isn't following too close."

"It's keeping its distance, about a block and a half behind me," Joe said. "There's a stop sign at the intersection ahead, correct?"

Kyle looked over at Erin, who glanced away from the GPS and nodded.

"Correct," Kyle affirmed. "I'll be coming up behind the van."

Before long, Kyle spotted the suspect's vehicle and slowed, keeping pace.

Erin used a pair of binoculars from Kyle's glove compartment to read the van's license tag. She wrote it down on a piece of notebook paper, then showed it to Kyle. He read it to the others.

"Roger that," Preston said. "Traffic around here is thinning out, so let's make our move. Jump lanes and take the next right as quickly as you can, Joe, but don't signal."

"We'll cut him off, and Kyle will close in from behind," Paul, riding with Daniel, added.

Kyle glanced quickly at Erin who was sitting up straight, anticipating the next few minutes. "Stay down," he said in a quiet, calm voice.

Ahead, Joe suddenly changed lanes and swerved onto the side street, taking the corner with squealing tires. Preston slammed on his brakes, then skillfully skidded sideways, blocking the road. Daniel tried to pull up even with the van, but the van quickly slowed, slipping behind Daniel's vehicle. In a bone-jarring move the driver leaped the median, and raced back in Kyle's direction.

"Hang tight!" Kyle yelled, cutting his speed, swerving the steering wheel to the left, and spinning completely around in a bootlegger's one-hundred-eighty-degree turn.

"We're going the wrong way!" Erin yelled.

"Not for long," Kyle replied. "Brace yourself."

Kyle edged to his right, leaped up onto the median with a thud, then dropped down onto the street, now only a half a block behind the fleeing van.

"Stay with him," Preston called over the radio.

The van was doing at least eighty-five down a city street, but there wasn't much traffic. Kyle had put on his blinkers and was leaning on his horn, trying to warn drivers out of the way.

When they reached Main Street, the van took a

chance and ran the light. "Can we make it?" Kyle asked Erin, whose eyes were everywhere searching for oncoming cars.

"We're clear."

They raced out of the city, up a two-lane road that led onto the south mesa and into the oil and gas fields that blanketed the Four Corners.

The van slowed as the highway curved right, and Kyle was able to close the gap. "Preston, what's your location?" he asked, not taking his eyes off the road.

"I'm bogged down. Emergency stop to avoid a TA. You on Route 135?"

"Affirmative. I'm closing in on the van. Where's Daniel?"

"Right behind me," Preston said. "We're caught between vehicles."

Erin looked over at Kyle, her eyes wide. "Now what?"

"We're not losing them again," he answered, wishing Erin were somewhere safe right now. What he really wanted to do was run those suckers off the road.

"He's slowing way down," Erin said, pointing ahead. "Why?"

The van's back door flew open, and bright lights flickered from inside.

Smudges suddenly appeared on the windshield accompanied by loud thumps. "Duck down, Erin."

Kyle was grateful for the bullet-resistant glass, but visibility was getting iffy. The front end rattled from a series of bullet strikes, then there was a loud whoosh.

"THAT SOUNDS BAD," Erin said, her voice shaky. "Did they hit the engine?"

Kyle looked down at the instrument panel. The temperature gauge was moving in the wrong direction—up. "They must have hit something in the radiator, taken out a hose or damaged the water pump."

"So this isn't a tank after all," Erin muttered.

"It's supposed to protect the passengers, not shoot it out with…" He almost said terrorists, but, then again, she'd heard that already.

"Preston, you still there?" Kyle asked.

His answer was barely audible over the engine sounds. "Yeah, what's happening?"

"My cooling system took a lucky hit. I'm close to redlining, and I'm losing speed—and the van," he said, watching the taillights ahead fade.

"Pull over before the engine seizes up. I'm trying to track down a helicopter to take up pursuit. I should be able to reach you in ten minutes or less. I'm losing you…."

"Preston? Daniel?" Kyle called out, then looked over at the display. Their signal was lost. The massive power lines paralleling the road here were interfering with the satellite relay.

Smelling the engine overheating and seeing steam rising from the hood, Kyle pulled over to the shoulder. Erin was sitting up now and staring out the side window.

"I can see the lights of the city back there somewhere, but nothing close. It's lonely out here," she said. "Think that van will turn around and come back for us once they realize we're out of commission?"

"I don't know," Kyle answered, wishing he could have sounded more reassuring. At the moment he could still make out taillights, which was a bad sign. "It looks like they've stopped, which means we can't stay here."

"If we just lock the doors…"

"They could set us on fire, and shoot us when we try to get out. We're vulnerable. Let's go."

They climbed out and Kyle retrieved his M4 assault rifle, along with the two extra magazines before locking up the SUV with his key fob.

"There's no cover close to the road, with the wide shoulders and the vegetation stripped from beneath the power lines. How about hiding among the trees over there?" Erin suggested, pointing across the road.

"Let's try to stick to our side of the highway. We don't want to go too far. It won't be long before help arrives. All we have to do is buy some time." He looked over at a large, flat rock surrounded by tall junipers, standing about twenty-five yards from the road.

"Climbing up on that rock is the obvious answer. We'd be able to see quite a ways up and down the road," he said. "Follow me and try to make sure your tracks are clearly visible. Stay on soft ground."

"Wouldn't it be smarter if we *hide* our tracks?" Erin asked, confused, then slowly smiled. "Wait a minute. I get it. The best defense is a good offense."

"You a history buff?"

Erin shook her head. "No, I just watch a lot of football."

FIVE MINUTES LATER they'd climbed up the front, and slid down the back of the big rock, leaving a well marked, false trail. Anyone tracking them would assume they were still up there, laying flat on their bellies on top of the rock.

As they moved to a different area, Kyle showed her how to rub out her tracks. Quickly, they made their way uphill until they reached hard sandstone. From there, they moved laterally to an area filled with junipers. Crouched low, they could still see the road and the false trail they'd left for whoever came after them.

They waited in silence, Kyle watching through the night scope on his M4. Soon they heard a vehicle moving slowly in their direction from up the road.

"It's the van, lights out," he whispered. Had he been alone, he would have gone down beside the rock and ambushed the perps, but he had someone to protect. Reinforcements were on the way and, for now, they were in the safest place he could find.

Two people got out of the van and jogged down the far side of the road, approaching within fifty feet of the SUV. They split up, circled the vehicle carefully, then, while one of them stood still, weapon aimed, the other approached the SUV and looked inside. He tried the door, failed to open it, then backed away, shaking his head. The second person turned in a slow circle, searching, then crossed the road.

"From the height and build, the smaller one's Frieda. I'm almost sure of it," Erin whispered.

Kyle looked through the scope again. If they came much closer, he'd have to start shooting, and he wanted to take at least one of the terrorists alive.

A man shouted from the van and the two on foot ran back toward the van, which drove up and met them halfway. In a heartbeat, the vehicle wheeled around and raced back up the road.

"I recognized that man's voice. It was gravelly, like Mike Bewley's," Erin said.

"The same guy Hank fired?" Kyle verified.

"Yeah."

"Let's go back to the SUV. The crew in that van won't be coming back. They either figured out we'd set up an ambush, or realized they were out of time."

"I can't believe Mike's involved with these creeps. I'd really hoped he'd figured out a way to put his own life back together."

Preston arrived just as they reached the SUV. "We managed to get in touch with a forest ranger driving in from the north and he spotted the van abandoned off the road a few miles farther up. They must have switched vehicles. Did you get a close look at the perps?"

"I think one of them was Frieda Martinez, the other, Mike Bewley," Erin said.

Preston looked at Kyle, as if waiting for confirmation.

"Neither one of us saw Frieda's face clearly, but the general physical description matched," Kyle said. "Erin identified Bewley based on his voice."

"I know that he used to drag race on weekends, too, and is real good behind the wheel," Erin added.

Kyle quickly gave Preston the rest of the details,

including their plan to ambush the two who'd left the van.

"What about the other guy, the one who went to check out your SUV?" Preston asked just as Daniel and Paul arrived.

"Even through the scope, I never saw him clearly enough to pick out his mug shot.

"For what it's worth, I want you to know that you handled today like a pro, Erin," Kyle said. "I couldn't have asked for a better partner."

She smiled slowly, and to Kyle, it felt as if she'd just lit up the darkness.

"There's something I still can't figure out," Preston said. "These terrorists are operating on *my* turf. What I want to know is how they're recruiting people without making any waves."

"There are always bottom feeders who can be bought."

"Like Mike Bewley," she said. "He needed money to crawl out of the hole he was in, and he hated Hank."

"Real revolutionaries tend to have a history that can be identified and traced. Their best soldiers are often people who've never been connected to the issue—people under the radar."

Preston's cell phone interrupted them. "Your phone works?" Kyle asked, surprised.

"Those big transmission lines are hell on satellite links, something about the frequency, but cell phones seem to work just fine," Preston said and answered the call.

Preston listened for several moments then spoke. "Keep an eye on him, and if he does anything illegal, bring him in. Call for backup if you need it."

"What's up?" Kyle said as Preston ended the call.

"New twist on the case," Preston said. "I've had an officer watching Erin's house. He just saw a man approach the front door, then go around when no one answered. He ran the plates on the truck, and it's Bruce Leland."

"How often does he come over to your place?" Kyle asked Erin.

"He dropped me off one time. That's it, but maybe he just wanted to talk to me about the business. Moe's out of town, remember?"

Preston answered his phone again. "I'm not buying it," he said. "Arrest Leland and bring him in. I'll meet you at the station."

"You're going to arrest him for going to my back door?" Erin asked, surprised.

"No, for B and E. He broke a rear window and crawled inside," Preston said.

"We'll follow you back to the station," Kyle told him, then glanced at Paul. "Looks like I'll need a full background on *all* the key players. Keep looking for any Spanish ecoterrorist connections. I want to find out who's running their operations here."

"I'll make it my top priority," Paul said.

Kyle looked at Erin and saw she was trembling now. Intending to comfort her, he walked to her side, but she stepped back.

"I'm not shaking 'cause I'm scared. I'm angry," she said, her eyes flashing. "If Bruce is involved with the people who murdered his brother, he has to answer for it."

Chapter Fourteen

Standing outside the interrogation room, Kyle pointed with his lips, Navajo style, at the man inside. "We're deliberately keeping the room hot to see if we can wear him down a little. In a while I'll go in and question him. You watch from here."

"Bruce has always seemed more pathetic than dangerous to me, but I was never afraid of him. Maybe I should have been," Erin whispered.

"I don't think he wanted to hurt you. He knew you wouldn't be home. Bruce was there to conduct a search."

"For the detonators Hank brought back from Spain?"

"What else could it be? The terrorists already have the explosives they need. They're going to do whatever's necessary to get those detonators now. They have a timetable to keep."

"I almost feel sorry for Bruce. He was manipulated and now just looks lost," she said, watching through the two-way glass.

"I hate to tell you this, but he fits the profile of someone recruited to betray his country—an individual looking for direction and someone to blame for being a failure," Kyle said. "Maybe you shouldn't watch this…."

"You don't want me to see you work?" she asked. "I know you have to be tough, and I can handle it. Innocent people have died, and that'll continue until you put a stop to it. Do what you have to do."

"All right, then," he said, then moved away to meet Preston.

"You sure you want her here?" Preston whispered. "What if she's been playing us all? Anything Leland says could end up being passed along to the wrong crowd."

"I trust my gut on this. Erin's the kind who's almost impossible to recruit," Kyle said. "She's motivated, a patriot who believes in the American Dream and is working within the system. No way she's with them."

"Okay, then. Let's go," Preston said.

They went into the interrogation room together. Kyle sat across the desk from Bruce while Preston remained standing, arms crossed in front of his chest.

"We've got enough to charge you for breaking and entering," Preston said, "but that's just the tip of the iceberg, Bruce. The people you're involved with are terrorists. They'll kill you the second they no longer need you. They don't leave loose ends."

"I don't know what you're talking about, but I wasn't breaking in. Well, I was, but I heard someone inside, calling for help. I thought Erin was in trouble."

Kyle's gaze was flat. "And you just happened to be in her yard when you heard that call for help from nobody? That's a lot of bull." He leaned over the table, getting into Bruce's face. "You're involved with terrorists planning an attack on our country. That makes you worse than a traitor," he said. "I'm here to give you the only chance you're going to get. Cooperate, and we'll do our best to keep you alive. Otherwise, the ones who murdered Hank will turn on you. They'll torture you until you give them what they want. Afterward, if you're lucky, they'll kill what's left of you."

"But I don't have them—" Bruce said, then stopped.

"You didn't get the shipment?" Kyle pressed, choosing his words carefully. He needed Bruce to incriminate himself.

"What shipment?" he said, his voice rising. "I'm telling you the truth, I don't know what's going on. All I can tell you is that Frieda convinced my brother to do her a favor when he was in Spain."

"*You* introduced them," Kyle said coldly.

"Yeah, I know. Frieda wanted to meet my

brother, said she wanted to work for his company. I told her Hank and I didn't get along and that I owed him some money. She offered to help me pay him back if I introduced her. She loaned me the money, too," he said, then added, "I didn't realize till later that she had her sights on Hank, not the job."

"What happened to the money she gave you?"

"I used it, but not to pay Hank, and that pissed her off. She'd wanted to use the fact that she'd loaned me money to put herself in Hank's good graces," he said. "Thing is, I had other, more pressing debts."

"Gambling?" Kyle asked.

"Yeah. I sold off everything I owned, squared most of the debt, and got some real bad people off my back."

"If she needed a job, didn't you wonder where she was getting the bucks to help you?" Kyle asked.

"Priorities, dude. My creditors had threatened to give me a real beatdown if I didn't come across with the cash."

"So you got involved with people who'll just as soon kill you instead," Kyle said. "Bad plan. The second they find out you've cooperated with us, you're as good as dead."

"What are you talking about?" Bruce's eyes widened. "I can't tell you what I don't know!"

"And you think they're going to believe that?" Kyle said, then shrugged. "Your funeral, guy."

Preston walked to the door. "While we process you for breaking and entering, you might want to think things over."

"One more thing," Kyle added. "When you finally leave the station, make sure you watch your back. These guys are everywhere, and they don't care what direction a man's facing when they kill him."

KYLE LEFT THE room and went to see how Erin had handled things.

She gave him a shaky smile as he approached. "I don't understand why Bruce isn't cooperating. The only choice he really has is to accept your help."

Kyle smiled. No recriminations, no disappointment, just a factual observation. Erin understood the nature of his work, and had taken it in stride. No wonder he was crazy about her. "In spite of all you've been through and seen, you can still stay focused. You'd make one helluva agent."

"If that's a compliment, thank you, but all things considered, I prefer agriculture."

He barked out a laugh. "I'll say this. You're the toughest farmer I've ever met."

"It goes with the job description," she answered,

then after a beat, added, "I miss it, you know. Watering in the morning, and all...."

"You'll get back to your life after this is over."

"That's just it. I'm not sure how much of my old life is left. Right now, I'm essentially unemployed. I still need to talk to Moe—"

Preston approached. "That's going to be tough, unless you have connections at the highest level," he said, and pointed heavenward. "Moe's dead."

"What?" she asked, and swallowed hard.

"How did it happen?" Kyle asked.

"Shot. We have the round. It came from a forty-five. Some tourists found his body beside one of the hiking trails in the Angel Peak Recreation Area."

"Who killed him? The same ones who went after Hank?" Erin asked in a shaky voice.

"We don't know yet," Preston answered. "The rounds we recovered so far have all been nine millimeter or .223 caliber."

"What about his paralegal, Ron Mora?" Kyle asked.

"Mora's also missing. Their office is locked up tight, and he's not home."

"Everyone connected to Hank is in danger now. That's true isn't it?" Erin asked.

"Yeah, that's my guess," Kyle said with a nod. "Erin, you knew Hank better than any of us. *Think.* What could he have done with those detonators?"

"I don't know!" she said. "I'm not holding out on you, Kyle. I have no reason to do that—unless you still think I'm part of this conspiracy." When neither man answered right away, her shoulders slumped. "I don't believe it. You're *not* sure, even after all this...."

"Until we have all the answers, we can't eliminate anyone," Kyle said, his voice gentling, "but instinct tells me you aren't involved. I wouldn't have turned my back on you if I felt differently, or let you listen in when I did."

"You knew I wasn't armed and, besides, I'm sure you know all kinds of Ninja stuff, and could have turned me into a pretzel," she said, giving him a tremulous smile.

"All true, but the fact remains I do trust you." He brushed his knuckles on her cheek. "We've been through a lot together, and I wouldn't lie to you."

"Without your help, I would have been dead by now," she said. "I may be terrified three-quarters of the time, but I'm also grateful for what you've done."

"No one will hurt you on my watch. Guaranteed."

"Kyle, I need to talk to you," Preston said.

"Wait here for me. I won't be long," he told Erin.

"My office is the second door to the left," Preston told her. "I brought that desert plant you were

worried about to my office. Go take a look at it
if you want."

"Thanks!" she said, her expression suddenly
brightening.

KYLE MET WITH Preston in the conference room,
then waited as Preston shut the door. "Okay, what's
up?" Kyle asked.

"You have to get that woman to trust you, Kyle,
and you're not making it happen. What's holding
you back? You losing your touch?"

"We've been a little busy dodging bullets."

"Bull. It's more than that...." He stared at Kyle,
and a second later, smiled. "Erin's getting to you.
You really like her."

"She's a witness and a person of interest. That's
all there is to it."

"But this time, you're the one with the interest.
You're keeping your distance because she's making you uncomfortable." He paused. "You need to
get Erin to open up to you, and to do that you'll
have to meet her halfway and tell her about yourself. She's going to have to trust you—not as a
federal agent, but as a man."

"Under other circumstances there would have
been time for that, but my priority has been a
trade-off between conducting an active investigation and keeping her alive."

"Why don't you take her to Copper Canyon? Daniel, Paul and I will work the leads while you take her out of the line of fire for a breather. That's the best chance you've got of jogging her memory."

Kyle nodded. His brother was right—on all counts. He had to help Erin figure things out. It could be the key to the entire investigation.

"I'll need transportation."

Preston handed him the keys to his own SUV. "Here you go."

As Preston was called to meet with his captain, Kyle went down the hall to his brother's office and saw Erin studying her plant, which was on a file cabinet near the window.

"It may be alive, but that's still the sorriest look-ing twig I've ever seen," he said, grinning to let her know he was teasing.

She chuckled. "I don't think it likes it here."

"I know a place it's bound to love."

"We're not going back to that horrible safe house again, are we?" she said, and shuddered. "Mabel needs sunlight, not fluorescent lamps and filtered air."

"You *named* the plant?"

"Yeah," she admitted, and to his surprise, she blushed.

"Then let's take Mabel with us," he said, chuck-ling. "I'm taking you to a very special place."

As THEY WALKED down the sidewalk toward the visitor's parking lot, Kyle positioned himself between her and the street and kept their pace brisk.

Right after two officers walked past them on the sidewalk, a large SUV pulling into the parking lot ahead caught Kyle's attention. Two young women dressed in office clothes climbed out, engaged in conversation. He relaxed slightly. For now, everything was as it should be.

"That poor lady," Erin murmured, watching an elderly woman crossing the street. She was leaning heavily on a cane, and pulling a small shopping cart filled with grocery bags. As she reached the curb, the old woman tripped and fell onto the sidewalk.

Erin immediately set the plant down on the hood of the closest vehicle and rushed over to help her.

"Erin, no, wait!"

As Erin bent down to lift the woman off the pavement, she reached up, grabbed Erin's collar and stuck a knife to her throat.

"Fancy meeting you here, Erin."

"Frieda?" Erin gasped, trying to pull away. "Are you crazy? What are you doing?"

"Hold still or you'll cut your throat." Frieda rose to full height, yanked Erin against her, and pulled her back toward the street.

As a big pickup roared around the corner, Frieda glanced back.

Kyle instantly lunged, his eyes never leaving the knife. In a lightning-fast move, he grabbed Frieda's knife hand. Palm out, he slammed her over the heart with his other hand, pushing her back hard.

As Frieda fell back onto the sidewalk, gasping, Kyle grabbed Erin. Wrapping his arms around her, he rolled under the closest SUV.

The pickup screeched to a stop a few feet away. "Get in," a voice called out to Frieda, then a door slammed shut.

Trapped beneath the vehicle, Kyle held on to Erin with one arm, his pistol in the other.

A heartbeat later the pickup raced off, tires squealing on the asphalt. The truck ricocheted off the curb and into the middle of the street, nearly colliding with an oncoming car before the driver recovered control.

By the time Kyle and Erin scrambled out from beneath the SUV, the pickup was already turning the corner at the far end of the block. Two officers were running after it, weapons out, but they gave up the chase without firing a shot.

"What was Frieda thinking? We're right next to the police station!" Erin said, her voice shaking.

"They're desperate, which makes them even more dangerous and unpredictable. Are you okay?" As he looked her over, he realized her gaze was fastened on the potted plant that had fallen to the sidewalk.

"That poor thing will never get a chance to bloom." She hurried over and scooped the dirt back into the plastic pot.

"Erin," Kyle said.

She refused to turn her head and Kyle knew she was crying. Flirting with death was part of his world, not hers.

"Darlin', hang on to that plant of yours. It's time to get going," he said, lifting her to her feet.

By then Preston arrived. "You two okay?" he asked.

Erin wiped her tears away quickly and nodded, but Kyle noticed that she had a death grip on her plant.

Preston gave Kyle a hard look. "I saw it go down from my window, so I'll handle the details. It's time for you to get going. Copper Canyon?"

Kyle nodded.

"I'll have the tribal P.D. increase patrols in the general area, so they'll be closer to you in case of trouble."

"No, don't," Kyle said. "More activity will pinpoint our location."

"Then consider changing your ride before you set out. Take Daniel's brown SUV. It's configured with the same enhancements as your agency vehicle—ballistic protection, GPS systems, the whole nine yards," he said. "Let me call him.

You'll like it. Dan can also provide you with an assault weapon with night vision."

Kyle called Daniel and arranged to meet him in front of the Quick Perk Coffee Shop, on his way out of town.

As THEY GOT underway in Preston's SUV, Kyle glanced over at the pot Erin was still holding. "That reminds me of a plant Hosteen Silver needed to grow for certain ceremonies. Its habitat was high up in the mountains on dry, rocky slopes, and it refused to grow anywhere else, but like you, he refused to give up on it," he said.

"What happened? Did your foster father find a way to make it grow?"

"Not at first. He tried growing it inside the house, but it died. He found another, planted it by the side of the house, blessed it, and then left it alone. A few weeks later, it began to spread like wildfire. It's super ground cover now, and nothing slows it down," he said. "He told us later that no one could tell the Plant People what to do. You had to show them respect and accept their decisions."

She glanced out the window. "It's true that forcing nature seldom works...."

"There's Daniel," Kyle said, interrupting her musings. "We'll need to switch vehicles as quickly as possible. I don't want us to linger outside one second longer than absolutely necessary."

She gathered the plant, and her purse. "Uh-oh. I just realized my clothes are still in your SUV."

"Then you'll wear mine. I've got plenty of stuff where we're going."

Chapter Fifteen

As they headed down the highway, his words played in her mind. It had been a practical gesture, but like a forbidden pleasure, the thought of wearing his clothes teased her imagination.

Trying to block out thoughts she knew were dangerous, she shifted her focus to Copper Canyon, a place she'd heard about growing up in the Four Corners but had never seen. She was looking forward to visiting the ranch that had made Kyle the man he was today.

They'd left the wide river valley, and were continuing west onto the Navajo Nation. The moonlit mesas here were scattered like giant tables extending above the upland desert plateau, all topped by junipers and piñon trees. Distant foothills led to the taller mountains beyond, spotted with forests of pine and fir.

"Is it much farther?" she asked after about an hour.

He laughed. "You sounded like I did the first

time Hosteen Silver brought me here. I must have asked him *are we there yet* a million times!"

"Where did you live before that, if not the rez?"

"I'd grown up in the city, Albuquerque, actually, and knew almost nothing about Navajo ways, but I had street survival down pat," he said. "If I needed cash, I could lift someone's wallet during an accidental bump. I also learned how to fight. I lost the first few, but before long, I could stand up to almost anybody."

It took a while for her to respond. "Don't think my parents would have liked me hanging around with you," she finally managed.

"I wouldn't have blamed them. I was a hard case, even at thirteen," he said. "If it hadn't been for Hosteen Silver, I'd probably be serving time right now instead of wearing a badge."

He'd turned south now, parallel to the mountains, and she realized she didn't quite know where they were any more. There weren't any lights visible anywhere except from the SUV—and the stars overhead.

Before long, they turned off the highway onto a dirt road that rose gently toward the tall cliffs ahead. After crossing an old wooden bridge, they passed through a narrow opening between two tall cliffs. They were now in a sagebrush, piñon and juniper woodland flanked on both sides by high mesas.

"Maybe you should slow down, Kyle. This road is getting pretty rough. If we high center and lose the oil pan it'll be a real long time before a wrecker arrives."

"Are you kidding, this is the best stretch of road," he said, chuckling. "Don't worry. I know every trail and arroyo in Copper Canyon. We're getting close to the ranch house now."

"It's so isolated, and closed off from the world. Are you really sure we'll be safe here?"

"It's a blind canyon. What makes the ranch house so safe is that there's only one way to approach by vehicle—the way we came in. The canyon transmits sound much like a tunnel, and you can hear someone coming before they're anywhere near," he said. "We're on reliable ground now, but if anyone tries to approach cross country in a wheeled vehicle, they'll bog down, high center, or find themselves blocked by a deep arroyo."

She rolled down the window. "It's eerily quiet out here."

"Once we're at the house, you'll be able to hear Copper Canyon's voice more clearly. Big cats hunt here, and deer and bears are frequent visitors. As for coyotes, they're everywhere. There's a lot of life here, and each has its own place within the pattern. There's room for all."

"You said you'd stayed here recently?"

"On my last vacation, I did. I came home to get my head together," he said.

"You said you were on your way to talk to Hank, but you never told me why. What made NCIS first take note of him?"

"Can't say."

She had no idea if that was true, or if he was just dodging the question. No matter how friendly Kyle seemed to be at times, he never completely lowered his guard.

As he maneuvered Daniel's SUV up a narrow path, she sat up. "Is that your home?" she asked, pointing ahead.

"Yeah, that's it."

Thanks to a bright full moon, she'd spotted the rectangular stucco framed house in the distance, not far from one of the tall cliffs. The house's metal roof shimmered in the moon's glow. Beyond that, about fifty yards from the house, was a log corral and small red barn.

"You have animals? I don't see any," she said.

"Gene keeps the horses at his ranch unless one of us is staying here. He'll bring a few down then so we can ride through the canyon," he said. "My brother Rick and I are the only ones who don't actually own a horse. We're not around enough for that."

"It would be hard to keep an animal when you're gone so much," she agreed.

"Lately, I've been giving some serious thought to coming home for good, and if I do, I'll buy a horse and board it at Gene's."

"Have you decided what you'd do for a living if you leave NCIS?"

"I could join Dan's company, or start my own, offering bodyguards for VIPs and the like. I wouldn't be competing with Dan, his thing is institutional and company security, but we could team up since we'd be offering overlapping services."

"That sounds interesting. What's holding you back?"

"It's a big career move, which means I'm going to need to work out a lot of details and come up with a solid business plan."

Kyle parked the SUV a short distance from the porch and led the way to the front door. After unlatching two strong-looking locks, he held up a hand. "Wait for me here while I look around inside."

A few moments later he returned. "Come on. I'll give you the guided tour."

Carrying her plant, she followed Kyle inside.

The small ranch house had a casual, rustic elegance. To her left was the kitchen, and in the center of that space was a large dining table and some straight-backed wooden chairs that had been hand carved using knotty pine.

Farther inside, she saw a sofa covered in rich

brown leather. The pine frame with its decorative grooves matched the design on the kitchen table and chairs. Beautiful red, black and indigo Navajo rugs were hung on the walls facing the big stone and iron fireplace.

"I love your home," she said, smiling as she placed the potted plant on the kitchen counter. "It welcomes you in a nonintimidating way, like a big, warm hug. Not at all like that safe house."

Kyle chuckled. "We've modernized this place in recent months, but the ranch house is meant to be a place where a man can kick off his boots," he said, then with a smile, added, "ladies, too."

"It definitely has that feel," she said, nodding. "I love that rug draped over the back of the couch. It looks different from the others and less bulky than the ones hung on the wall."

"That's an antique given to Hosteen Silver in payment for a Sing. It's a blanket, not a rug. Almost everything woven by my tribe before 1890 is a blanket. Navajos began weaving floor coverings for the tourist trade around that time because there was such a high demand."

She looked at the fireplace. "Gas fireplaces are so popular these days, but I've always loved the wood-burning kind, like this one. With the scent of pine and rosin, and the snapping and popping of burning sap, they're more...I dunno. Romantic?"

"Remind me to light it for you," he said. "At

night it gets cold in this canyon, and there's no heating system, just that."

"In winter, that must be tough."

"Not really. The house is very well insulated, and the fireplace itself is constructed with ducts and openings to distribute heat with great efficiency. My brothers and I have also spent a lot of time getting things up-to-date here. We have hot and cold running water now and electricity, too. The wires are below ground and the power provided allows us to run heat tape so that the pipes don't freeze and our hot-water heater keeps working."

"I'm glad to hear that," she said. "I'm not into ice-cold showers. In that respect, I'm a complete wuss."

"Lady, you're anything but that," he answered, leading her down the hall. "We have three small bedrooms, but one's used as storage, so you've got a choice of two."

"You'll be next door, right?"

"No, tonight I'm going to take the sofa. I'd rather stay in the front room. From there I can see both front and back doors."

"You think they'll find us?" she asked, her voice rising.

"Probably not, but I'm not going to lay back and hope for the best."

She walked to a hand-carved desk that stood in

one corner of the main room. There was a closed notebook on its surface, and the beautiful handwriting on the label affixed to it caught her attention. "Is this your work?"

He shook his head. "That's Hosteen Silver's journal. None of us have opened it and looked inside yet. He recorded his thoughts in there, along with details of his special Sings and personal observations. He could have destroyed it before his death, but he left it where he knew we'd see it for a reason." Kyle walked over and stared at it, but didn't touch it. "Reading it will feel like invading his privacy."

"But if he left it for you…"

"I know, and that's what's puzzling. Most Navajos are taught to avoid the personal possessions of the dead. To tamper with them is to risk angering the chindi."

"His ghost?"

"No, that's not what a chindi is, not exactly anyway. Traditionalist Navajos believe that the good in a man merges with universal harmony, but the evil side gets left behind. Earthbound, it lies in wait, hoping to create problems for the living." He paused. "Hosteen Silver would have made sure that it was safe for us to handle, but reading his most private thoughts…"

"Will be hard," she said, understanding. "You'll

risk finding out things you never wanted to know, and that might destroy the way you remember him."

"That's why my brothers and I decided to wait until we were all present to read it. Rick's still out of the country."

"Is he in law enforcement?"

"Yeah, he's with the FBI, but none of us know exactly what his job is. We've asked, but all he ever says is that it's above our pay grade," Kyle said.

"So it's a family thing—keeping secrets," she said, teasing him.

He chuckled. "You may be right about us—all except for Gene, that is. He's a rancher, and with him, what you see is what you get."

"Why not just leave the journal closed—a mystery?" she asked, and saw his face cloud over.

"That's not an option. The death of our foster father left us with a lot of unanswered questions. That journal may give us some closure," he said. "Of course it could also open new wounds."

For the first time, beyond the hardness of his gaze, she could see vulnerability. Kyle was a strong man, but he wasn't impervious to pain.

"Tell me more about growing up here in Copper Canyon," she asked gently. "The transition couldn't have been easy."

"It wasn't, but I handled it," he said, his eyes hooded again.

She remained silent for a moment. "My question obviously crossed a line, and that wasn't my intention, but here's the problem, Kyle. I'm not even sure where the line is! Tell me this much. Do you care for me at all, or am I just part of your job?"

"You're really asking me that after the way I kissed you?"

His deep voice sent its vibrations all through her. For a moment she almost forgot to breathe. "What you were offering me wasn't love or friendship. It was a one-night stand."

"Who's to say that one can't lead to the other?" he said, moving close enough for her to feel the heat from his body.

Her heart was lodged in her throat. "You're doing this to avoid answering my question." Somehow she held her ground and forced herself to look him in the eye. "Sex is easy for you—friendship isn't."

"Maybe," he said, and moved back, giving her more room. "When you grow up like I did, you learn fast that it doesn't pay to let anyone get too close."

She reached for his hand and held on to it. He appeared unbreakable, but only because he'd learned to hide the cracks in his armor. For the first time she began to understand him.

"I know what it's like to have your heart ripped out. When my marriage fell apart, I had no one to turn to. I had to stand on my own and find a way to survive," she said. "If there's one person you can count on never to betray you, it's me. I care about you. I really do."

He kissed her hand gently, then let it go. "You're following your heart but, sweetheart, I'm a bad bet."

"I know," she said, not bothering to argue the point.

Erin stepped back and looked away, searching for a distraction. That's when she saw that the potted plant she'd left on the counter was leaking soil. "The pot's cracked," she said, hurrying over. "It must have taken a harder fall than I realized. Do you have something I can put Mabel in?"

"There's a shed beside the barn," he said. "If we have any flower pots, they'll be in there."

Taking a lantern from the table, he led the way to the small building beside the barn. Kyle opened the locked shed door. There were cans of paint, tools and other supplies they'd used to update the ranch house, but nothing suitable for Mabel.

"I'm sorry," he said at last. "How about a big bowl from the cupboard?"

"There won't be any drainage. We need something else. I can't just let it die," she said, taking a shuddering breath. "Mabel is all about keeping the

faith and about not giving up." She swallowed hard
to keep from crying. "I sound deranged, right?"
she added with a weak smile.

"No, darling, you don't." He picked up a shovel
and gestured toward the house. "Let's go. We'll put
it in the ground. I know the perfect spot. It'll get
light almost all day, and when it rains, the water
collects there."

"Where Hosteen Silver's bush now grows?"

He nodded and smiled, leading the way. "Yes.
His plant is called oak-under-a-tree and only grows
to be about six inches tall. It's great ground cover,
so it'll also help keep the soil around the rose moist
whenever it rains," he said. "Most important of all,
oak-under-a-tree is a good luck plant."

Setting the lantern down where it would illu-
minate the area, he dug a hole.

Erin carefully planted Mabel, then shaped the
soil around it into a small basin so that water
would collect around its roots.

"There," she said at long last. "That's all we
can do."

"One more thing." He reached into the leather
pouch she'd seen him wearing around his neck,
brought out a pinch of something, then scattered
it over the plant. "Pollen is a symbol of light and
life. It'll bless your plant."

A moment later his voice rose in a haunting,
monotone chant that seemed to reverberate with

power and a gentleness she wouldn't have associated with Kyle.

When he finished, she looked at him with new wonder. "That was beautiful."

"It's something I remembered, a *hozonji,* a song that brings luck."

"Thank you," she said. The fact that he'd understood and respected what the plant meant to her, and that he'd tried to help insure its survival, had touched her in a way that she hadn't expected. "Kyle, you're full of surprises."

Chapter Sixteen

They went back inside as thunder began rumbling in the distance, accompanied by distant streaks of lightning. "It looks like we'll have rain tonight," he said.

"The weather's really cooled off, too. Will you build a fire and then tell me about your leather pouch?"

"Sure, but first I have to split some logs, then we'll bring in some kindling and firewood."

"I can help carry them back in."

"Sounds fair. I chop. You carry," he said. "There's a firewood carrier under the overhang of the barn by the woodpile."

They returned outside and Erin held the lantern while he began splitting wood on an old pine stump. Cutting through the thick logs with powerful strokes seemed effortless to him.

Then as he raised his axe again, his shirt flew open and something flew outward, landing in the dirt. "I just lost three buttons," he said. "That's what I get for trying to wear Dan's shirts. Puny son of a gun."

She laughed, knowing that Daniel was anything but that. However, in all fairness, none of the brothers she'd met so far had Kyle's build. He was broad in all the right places, and narrow where it counted.

He stripped off his shirt, found the missing buttons, then walked over to her. "Hang on to these for me while I finish, will you?" Then, taking the medicine pouch from around his neck, he gave that to her, as well.

She stood back, enjoying the view. His shoulder muscles rippled and his stomach tightened as he swung the axe. He was a thing of beauty—all male and a temptation to any woman who still drew breath. She could feel her hands tingling with the need to touch him.

"I'm almost through. How about you? Had enough?" he asked, then gave her a thoroughly masculine grin. "I'm not shy, so if you want a more thorough look, I'll be happy to oblige."

She sucked in her breath. "I wasn't staring."

"Like hell."

"Okay, busted. Now come on," she added, quickly diverting him. "Let's carry the wood inside. It's starting to rain. Can you—"

At that precise moment the skies seemed to open up and sheets of rain descended.

They loaded the metal carrier, then hustled inside as fast as they could.

"You're a native New Mexican, so you know storms like this don't last. They come on strong, it rains like mad for fifteen minutes, then it's over." He grabbed a couple of towels from the linen closet in the hall and tossed her one.

"Take one of my shirts from the bedroom on the left. It's around fifty degrees inside the house right now, so you'll need dry clothes."

"I'll be okay once you build a fire," she said, returning the buttons and medicine pouch. "What got the wettest is my hair." She glanced out the window as she towel-dried it. "Do you ever get flooded here at the low end of the canyon?"

"Not really." Kyle placed the kindling on the fireplace grate. "Hosteen Silver chose this place carefully. After a heavy rain, the intermittent stream that forms passes out of the canyon west of the road. Just to make sure we'd always be safe, he also buried earth bundles filled with soil from the sacred mountains in all four corners of the house. That soil is particularly powerful because those mountains are said to be the forked hogans of the gods. When the spring winds rip through here and branches and trees topple over, they always seem to fall away from the house, too," he said. "I can't explain it logically, but when Hosteen Silver blessed something, you could count on results."

"That also explains why you and your brothers turned out so well." Her gaze strayed over him, enjoying that perfect moment. The fire now roaring in the fireplace made his copper skin glow and accentuated his muscular build.

He smiled. "Come over here."

She hesitated, but he looked so sexy shirtless, she just couldn't resist. She wanted to touch him, to feel his naked skin against her palms.

"Touch me, I don't bite," he said, his voice husky. "You're safe. All I want is one kiss in return."

She should have run. This man could make her yearn for things she had no business wanting. Yet something inside her refused to take the safe road and back away.

She touched his chest gently, taking pleasure in skimming her palms over him, loving the way his muscles rippled under her touch. He was all hard planes and ridges. His jeans hung low, so she trailed a finger down his chest all the way to the lower part of his stomach.

She heard him draw in his breath. "You're not as controlled as you want me to believe." Looking up at him, she saw the heat mirrored in his gaze.

"Nothing will happen, just one kiss."

She stepped closer to him and lay her head

against the crook of his neck, loving the way their bodies fit together.

His hand curled into a fist as he struggled for control. Tucking it beneath her chin, he lifted her face toward his and kissed her, his mouth moving tenderly over hers, coaxing her lips to part.

She soon lost track of everything except the hazy wave of pleasure that was coursing through her. The deeper and the rougher his kiss got, the more she surrendered to those forbidden pleasures.

She didn't want to stop. She'd never needed anything, or wanted anyone, more than she did him. Hunger, yearnings…was she falling in love?

The thought frightened her and stopped her cold. She wedged a hand between them and stepped back. She wouldn't give herself to a man who didn't love her, and who'd leave her as soon as his work was done. Promises whispered in the dark died in the light of day, breaking the heart and spirit. She deserved more—and so did he, though he probably didn't realize it.

"That was an incredible kiss," she said, still struggling to catch her breath.

"It doesn't have to end. There are other places I could kiss."

Her knees nearly buckled. Her entire body felt electrified and sensitive to even the heat of his breath. She moved back another step.

"I don't play at love, Kyle. I don't know if the

real thing will ever find me, but I won't settle for an imitation, or a temporary substitute." As she walked away from him, he focused on stoking the dying flames in the fireplace.

He took a seat on the hearth as she sat down on the sheepskin rug near the fire.

"You want to know more about me, and I get that, but it's hard for me to talk about myself," he said. "Let's give things another try. Ask me whatever you want."

"Tell me something, anything, I don't already know about you," she said.

"My mom died giving me birth and my dad died six years later in a mining accident."

"But you didn't go live with Hosteen Silver until you were thirteen?"

He nodded. "At first I was taken in by my uncle, but he didn't want a kid around, particularly me. He said I'd been bad luck from day one."

"That's a horrible thing to tell a kid," she said angrily. "An adult can deal with that kind of rejection, but a six-year-old kid hasn't learned to put up solid defenses."

"Like I said, I had to grow up fast."

"I'm glad Hosteen Silver eventually found you."

"I didn't make things easy for him, though. I was a handful back then."

She smiled. "You're a handful now."

He laughed. "You think so, do you?"

She looked around the main room and smiled. "This looks like a terrific place to grow up."

"When I first came out here, it wasn't nearly so comfortable. The ranch house had few modern conveniences. There was no electricity and we had to haul water for the horses and the sheep. That, by the way, is one of the toughest jobs in the world," he said. "One time after working all Saturday on chores, I got angry and told Hosteen Silver that the only reason he'd fostered us was 'cause he wanted money from the state and free labor."

"How did he react?"

"He told me to grow up, that any able-bodied man who was worth a damn was capable of doing a day's work to earn his keep," Kyle answered. "He was trying to teach me respect for honest labor, but at that point, I was a kid used to doing pretty much whatever I wanted. To me, it all hinged on who could stop me, and whether it was worth the fight." He paused, then added, "I owe him everything. My brothers, too."

As lightning crashed nearby, she jumped. "Wow, that was close!"

"You afraid of lightning?"

She shook her head. "Not afraid, I just don't like it striking so close. It's loud and angry. It destroys, causes fires… I see nothing good in it."

"I've always enjoyed watching thunderstorms. It's nature's light show," he said, pulling her to her feet. Turning off the lamps, he led her to the kitchen-area window that offered a clear view of the upper canyon, and stood behind her as they watched the sky.

There was a bright flash overhead, followed only a few seconds later by a loud clap of thunder that shook the house and rattled the windows. She sucked in her breath.

Kyle wrapped his arms around her and held her close. "It's raw power—defiant and unpredictable," he whispered in her ear, "but if you accept it for what it is, and use caution, it can't harm you."

"Some things are better avoided."

"Maybe, but you'll miss a lot of life that way."

"Some people rush toward danger, others duck and take cover. Given the choice, I prefer ducking," she said with a tiny smile. "Good thing you don't, considering your job."

"I love my work," he said, moving her gently to one side of the window, probably so they wouldn't present the perfect targets to anyone outside. "But once this case is wrapped up, I'll have to see where things stand for me. If there's a specific reason I'm still needed at NCIS, I'll stay till the work's done. I never run out on people who are counting on me."

"What if they always need you?" she asked, leaning back and enjoying the warmth of his chest and arms, which were wrapped securely around her.

"That won't happen. My usefulness is limited.

I've seen…too much. Burned out, some would say."

"Something happened to you and it changed everything, didn't it?" she asked. When he didn't answer, she turned in his arms and faced him. "Sometimes it helps to talk things over, and I'm the perfect person for you to use as a sounding board."

"How so?"

"I'm only going to be in your life for a short time. Sharing your secret can't change anything between us," she said, stepping back.

"I'm not sure if I agree with that. Once I'm home, we could see each other as often as we like."

She walked over to the fireplace, enjoying its warmth. She wanted to cling to the hope that, against all odds, things would work out between them.

"What are you thinking?" he asked when she didn't answer.

"Holding back is second nature to you, but what you don't seem to understand is that I would never judge you—no matter what."

"The world I've lived in is nothing like life here in Hartley. I'm not sure you can handle this."

"When you rescued me our lives became intertwined. How long that will last, who can say? But here's what I do know," she said, cupping his face in her hands and meeting his gaze. "No matter what's in your past, I know who you are right now. If falling down along the way made you who you are today, then it was worth it."

He pulled her into his arms and held her tightly for a brief eternity. Then, as the downpour continued outside, he released her.

Erin returned to the sheepskin rug by the fire and sat down. In his arms she'd known warmth, but now, despite her proximity to the flames, it felt as if the temperature in the room had dropped ten degrees.

"I'm going to trust you, Erin, not because I have to, but because I want to," he said. "Before I begin, I'll need your word that you won't ask me where I was, or anything specific about my mission. Agreed?"

She nodded.

He began to pace restlessly around the room, but it took several minutes before he finally spoke. "I was on assignment overseas, deep undercover and under orders to cultivate some sources so I could gather intelligence. Before long, I found a young man about sixteen who worked pumping gas and selling cooking fuel to those with stoves at home. He'd taken the business over from his father, a mechanic, who was disabled. It was just the two of them."

"Someone with such an ordinary job was important to you?"

"I was trying to find out who in the village was working with terrorists, making smuggling runs involving stolen navy ordnance and communications equipment. Since that would require a lot of extra fuel, I figured the boy might have the answers I needed."

He said nothing for a long moment, continuing to pace, then began again.

"I knew the boy's father was in a great deal of pain from his disability, so I went up the chain of command and arranged for him to get the medications he needed. Soon after that, he began to walk again and resumed working with his son. They were both very grateful and, in return, gave me access to their records. From the fuel outlays and customer lists, I was able to get all the information I needed."

"So you succeeded," she said.

"Yes, but in the meantime, word traveled fast and a local warlord heard what I'd done. One morning I dropped by early and was there talking to the son as his father approached on foot. Before he could join us, two men on a motorcycle stopped to talk to him and the three began to argue. I held back, thinking it was a private matter. I didn't want to make things worse by intervening."

He turned away from her, and stared outside. "I was less than fifty feet away when one of the men grabbed something from the boy's father and pushed him back hard. I drew my weapon, but by then it was too late. They gunned him down right in front of his son."

Erin drew in a sharp breath and covered her mouth with one hand.

"I shot one of the assailants, but the other raced away on the motorcycle," Kyle said in a monotone. "The father was dead by the time we got to him. On the ground, between the father and the gunman, was a broken vial of painkillers."

He turned and met her gaze. "They killed him because he had those pills. If I hadn't interfered, using them as sources, that man wouldn't have died."

"That wasn't your fault. You had no idea what was going to happen," she said. "Did the boy understand that?"

Kyle shook his head. "He held me responsible and insisted I leave immediately and never come back. I left, but I set up a post some distance away and kept watch on the garage, thinking the same people would return and kill the boy, too. Later that night, I saw the garage catch fire. A case of arson, I found out later. I ran back in and got the boy out, but it was clear that he couldn't stay in the area anymore. He had to be taken to a new village far away from his relatives and extended family. That was a huge loss in that part of the world." He paused. "Eventually I found the ones responsible

for what happened, but the price the boy paid…
that was beyond my power to fix."

"You acted out of compassion and did the right
thing. You can't take the blame for the actions
of others," she said, going to where he stood and
wrapping her arms around him.

He gathered her against him and held her tightly.
For several long moments neither said a word. "I
care for you, Erin, more than you know."

"Then show me," she whispered.

She felt his body grow hard, and even though
she understood the danger, an instinct rooted in
nature itself kept her where she was. He was in
pain, the kind that tore straight to his soul. He
needed her…and she needed him.

He kissed her hard, dragging her head back and
ravishing her mouth. He was rough, but knowing
how badly she was needed and wanted made it all
the more exciting.

"More," she whispered.

Heat bound them together. He was out of control, but she invited everything and resisted nothing.

"I've fantasized about this…." she murmured.

He helped her undress, kissing her as she did,
slowly driving her crazy with needs, determined
to make tonight be better than any fantasy.

"Lie down for me," he said, helping her onto
the sheepskin rug.

Standing before her, he undid his belt and stripped.

Her breath caught in her throat. He was magnificent. "Tonight is about you and me—nothing else," he growled.

As he came to her, she opened her arms, welcoming him. His body was taut, but he took his time, his touch impossibly gentle as he caressed her.

Like nature's show outside, where darkness danced with light, there were no barriers or rules. He began to teach her things she'd never known, leading her to a place where fire ruled.

It wasn't until afterward that he realized what had happened. He'd never lost control like that, but then again, he'd never been in love.

Hours passed, but he remained where he was. She was lying on his chest, listening to his heart and he didn't want to move. He liked the feel of her against him. It was where she belonged.

He kissed her forehead gently. "I'd like to stay here, but I have to go outside and take a look around."

She sat up and reached for her shirt. "Time for work," she said with a nod.

Seeing the disappointment in her eyes, he fought the temptation to lie back down and take her again.

Instead, he got dressed quickly. "I'll stay on the couch tonight."

"Where should I sleep? Do you have a preference?"

"Take my bedroom and sleep easy, sweetheart. I'll watch over you," he said, kissing her gently.

Before she could answer, he turned away and walked out the door.

ALONE AGAIN, ERIN finished getting dressed. She'd never forget tonight, not for as long as she lived. In his arms, she'd discovered a side of herself she'd never known existed. Following her heart, she'd come alive and entered a world of passion. She smiled thinking of her mother. Somehow, she knew Rita Barrett would have approved.

Kyle would break her heart some day, there was no doubt about that. Yet some things were worth the price they exacted. She had no regrets.

Chapter Seventeen

Erin slept in Kyle's bed wearing one of his flannel shirts. It was way too big and hung down to her knees, but she'd never slept so soundly.

She awoke after daybreak, hearing him moving around. Dressing quickly, she went to join him.

Kyle was on the phone, but smiled at her as she came into the room and pointed to a carafe of coffee on the kitchen counter.

She went over and poured herself a cup, all the time wishing she could ask him even one of the million questions still running through her mind. Had last night been a life-changing event for him as it had for her, or just another encounter in the dark?

She brushed the thought aside. Love, the real kind, didn't come with demands or ultimatums. Its roots were in freedom.

"I have difficulty believing that they've gone so far underground we can't find them," Kyle snapped. "They didn't follow us here. That much

I know, and I'll make sure I don't pick up a tail on our way back," he said, ending the call.

"Preston hasn't been able to locate Frieda Martinez, but he did some digging and found out Frieda and the bartender at the Quarter Horse Bar, Ed Huff, had a thing," Kyle told her. "His informant said it ended over a year ago, though. Now Ed Huff appears to have gone missing, too. He hasn't reported to work in two days. The owner's furious."

"Then let's go back to Secure Construction. That's where this all began. The answers must be there somewhere," she said.

"Preston suggested that, too, but we'll have to stay sharp every step of the way. They'll be watching for us."

Despite her best efforts, she began to tremble.

Seeing it, he pulled her into his arms. "Listen to me, and listen good. No way they're going to lay a hand on you. This is my turf and the home team has the advantage. My brothers have my back and I'm right here to protect you. I'm hard as hell to kill, too, which is what they'll have to do to get anywhere near you."

"You'll be there, no matter what," she said.

"Yes. No matter what."

"All right." She took a deep breath, and thought back to her last conversation with her boss.

As they set out, she lapsed into a long, thought-

ful silence. They were back on the highway, on secure, solid ground, when she spoke again. "Hank
was a bit of a control freak. He made me manager,
but I still had to check everything I did with him.
He wasn't the kind to share responsibility."

"So would you say that his business was the
single most important thing to him?"

She considered it. "No. I'd say it was his reputation. He liked being considered one of Hartley's
leading citizens—or at least, a success. That's why
I don't see him as a smuggler, Kyle, especially
with something so dangerous and un-American.
It would have gone against his nature, do you understand?"

"Yes, but that need to protect his reputation
would have made him even more susceptible to
blackmail."

"Had he known he was shipping back detonators, he would have refused. Look what happened once he dismantled those electronic tools
and found out what they held. His sense of duty
took over immediately," Erin said.

"And he did what he could to undo the mess he
was in, hoping he could make things right somehow," he said with a thoughtful nod. "Let's say
he expected them to come looking for the detonators. He didn't know how much time he had so
he needed to hide them fast." He paused. "Erin,

those detonators are on his turf. That would fit in with his need to control the situation, too."

"Your brother and his team already went through Hank's home, right?"

"Yeah, and Preston is very thorough. If he says they're not at the house, you can count on it. He looked through the office, too, even with dogs trained to sniff out explosives."

"There are lots of places to hide things over at Secure Construction. The yard alone is huge. Then there's the warehouse. It could take months to go through absolutely everything."

"That's what worries me. We don't have that much time. It's Friday. The dedication ceremony is the day after tomorrow."

She expelled her breath in a hiss. "Hank was incredibly security minded. Going from that standpoint, I have an idea."

SHE REMAINED QUIET for the most part as they rode back to Hartley. Giving her time to think, he didn't interrupt the long silence.

Kyle kept his eyes on the road and on the rearview mirror, but the elusive flowery scent that clung to her was making him crazy. It was soft, like her cries last night as he'd given her pleasure.

He'd been with a lot of women throughout his life, but with Erin everything had been different.

What they'd shared hadn't been a one-off, not in his mind anyway.

He shook free of those thoughts. No more distractions. He had to focus on protecting her.

They stopped for coffee and a bag of doughnuts, then about twenty-five minutes later, arrived in Hartley.

"You haven't said much the past fifty miles. Are you ready to share your thoughts?" he asked.

"Yeah. There's a small safe room in the warehouse. It was Hank's favorite haunt. Whenever he wanted to do without interruptions, he'd tell me to hold his calls, then he'd head over there."

"We'll search there first," he said, and made a hard left.

"Whoa! Where are you going? Secure Construction is to the right," she said, grabbing the arm rest for balance.

"I need to make sure we haven't picked up a tail." He looked in the rear and side mirrors. "Okay, we're good for now, but stay sharp."

"I will."

"One more thing. This is only a precaution, but I'd like you to carry this with you at all times." Reaching into the pocket of his jacket, he brought out a plastic button.

"This is more than just a button, right?"

"Yes, it contains a GPS tracker. Should we ever get separated, I'll find you," he said, switching it on. Pointing to the computer screen in the car, he showed her the signal. "Carry it somewhere where there's no chance you'll lose it."

"Like where? Tucked in my bra?"

He slipped the leather cord from around his neck and handed it and the attached pouch to her. "Take out the fetish and give it back to me, then put the GPS inside the pouch and keep it around your neck on the cord. Make sure it's out of sight, like inside your shirt."

"You were going to tell me about your pouch and the fetish yesterday, but we got sidetracked," she said with an impish smile.

"That's one way to put it," he said, chuckling.

She pulled out the tiny carving. "Is it a fox?"

"Yes," he said. "The fetish was a special gift from Hosteen Silver. All my brothers have a different guardian animal, one whose spirit matches their character. According to our traditionalists, the right combination can enhance the abilities of the person who carries it. For example, Fox's attributes are intelligence and observational skills. Fox helps me find answers even when none are apparent."

"What an interesting gift," she said.

"And a powerful one, too. I never thought much about it back then, but over the years I learned how to use it. Fox is my spiritual brother. When I focus on Fox's spirit and go about my business, positive results invariably follow."

"Maybe someday I'll get my own fox," she said.

"You have one already," he said, and gave her a wink.

"I meant a fetish," she said, chuckling.

He grew serious. "Fox wouldn't be right for you. Your spiritual sister will have to be an extension of who you are."

"Since I have the cord and the pouch, where will you keep your fetish?"

"This is my brother's SUV. He's no traditionalist, but I'm betting that if you reach into the glove compartment, there's a pouch there."

She did and found one all right. "What's inside this one, a different fetish?"

"No. That one will have pollen, a crystal and a tiny sprig of Rocky Mountain juniper, another good luck plant, for protection."

"I know what pollen signifies, but what does the crystal represent?"

"During creation, our gods placed a crystal in the mouth of each person so that their prayers would always be heard," he explained. "Mixed with pollen, a symbol of well-being, the prayer also becomes a blessing."

Kyle used one hand to place the fox in the larger pouch, then looped the leather cord around his neck.

"We're all set then," she said.

They pulled up to the closed gates shortly thereafter. The first thing Kyle noticed was that there were no noncompany vehicles visible and the gates were locked.

"Don't worry. I've got a key," she said.

"The fact it's just us will work to our advantage," he said, taking her key. "No interruptions or explanations needed." He went to open the gate.

After driving through and closing the gate behind them, Kyle's car phone beeped. He saw it was his brother, and answered, putting it on speaker. "I'm here."

"I know. I've got your GPS," Preston said. "I drove by the business earlier and verified that no one's on site. Bruce Leland, who has the best claim at ownership at the moment, told the work crew to finish up their current job then wait for further news before they come back in. The payroll checks have to be countersigned by the attorney, but since he's dead, things are at a standstill."

"Any word on Ron Mora?" Erin asked. "I sure hope he's okay. He's a really nice guy."

"Turns out that he was using an assumed identity, so he's not so nice, Erin. His social security number belongs to a dead infant and was stolen from a government database by a hacker," Preston said.

"So who *is* Ron?" she asked.

"Your guess is as good as ours. We lifted prints from his desk, but have nothing so far, despite sending copies to the feds, plus Spanish law enforcement. It also turns out that Ron doesn't have a driver's license on file."

"How did he manage to get a position working for Moe Jenner?" Kyle asked.

"With Jenner dead, we're not likely to get that answer right away."

"Keep on that," Kyle said, "and the minute you find out anything, let me know."

"Copy that. One more thing. Do you plan to stick around there for a while?"

"Yeah, I locked the gate behind us, but having some extra people in the area would be good," Kyle said.

"You've got it," Preston answered.

After he hung up, Kyle glanced around one more time. He'd parked out of view of the main street. "Let's get out and take a look around."

As they entered the warehouse, Kyle noted how quiet Erin had become. "Is something wrong?"

"It's Bruce. Even if he's the closest relative, he really shouldn't be making decisions for the company."

"Then who should?"

"The will specified what Hank wanted done, so I think everyone should respect that until we can find a new attorney."

"Legal questions can take a long time to be settled," Kyle warned.

"I know, but still…"

Kyle followed her across the warehouse to a self-contained room in the back. She stepped aside and waved him in.

"This is the safe room we show clients," she said. "It's not connected to any other walls so inside and outside construction details can be examined. Having this here gives people a feel for what it's like inside one of our models. The four walls are reinforced and it's impossible for anything short of an armor-piercing round to penetrate them, much less a cinder block tossed around by a tornado. All our designs meet the Federal Emergency Management Agency's criteria."

She stepped to the fold-down table connected to one wall. "Once you close the door, you have complete privacy and soundproofing. Hank almost always worked on the next quarter's projections in here."

Kyle ran his hands over the chair legs, and the table, lifting it up enough to look underneath. "Not here."

She sat down on the small sofa. "He used to like this particular spot. He'd lean back and think things through," she said, imitating the position Hank favored.

Kyle examined the sealed walls and ceiling for any seams or concealed compartments but found nothing.

Turning around, he watched the way she was sitting. "Check your line of sight when you lean back like that," he suggested.

He saw her focus on something just beyond the door and tried to figure out what had her attention. "What are you looking at?" he asked after a moment.

"The mower's stored exactly where it should be, but the canvas bag used to gather grass clippings is missing," she said.

"Let's look around for it. My gut's telling me you may be onto something."

They searched the warehouse, then walked across the graveled compound toward the office, which was surrounded by a small lawn. Concrete pavers had been spaced across the grassy expanse, creating a walkway.

As they got closer, he stopped and pointed. "Two pavers are missing," he said, "and based on the impressions still there, they haven't been gone very long."

"That's odd. Who'd steal something like that? They're just dead weight."

"The night Hank flew back, I followed him here from the airport. He spent quite a bit of time in his office, and also went in and out of the warehouse twice. I couldn't get close enough to see what he was up to without being seen. After about an hour he left the compound and headed home.

He took the long way, using the less traveled old highway and the steel trestle bridge, but at the time I chalked it up to him wanting to make sure he wasn't being followed. Now I think he had another plan in mind."

"I get it. You're thinking that he put the detonators in the grass clipping bag, used the pavers for weight, and dropped the bag into the river," she said.

Kyle started to answer, then stopped, and signaled her to be quiet. A heartbeat later, he pulled her into the shadows of the building. The gate had rattled, which meant that someone had just climbed over it.

They were no longer alone.

Chapter Eighteen

Kyle remained perfectly still. Someone else had come into the compound. As if to confirm his suspicions, he heard the crunch of gravel somewhere close.

"Focus on me, and do exactly as I say," he told Erin in a harsh whisper.

They walked quickly down the side of the building to the rear, then jogged across the gap between the office and one of the garages. Trying to lead whoever was following them into an ambush, he made enough noise on the gravel to be heard.

After circling the building, he pulled her down behind a row of sand-filled fifty-five-gallon drums used to create a vehicle barrier for security demonstrations. Looking past her for a second, he pointed to a shovel leaning against the wall of the building.

She reached back and handed it to him.

He then motioned for her to crouch low to the ground. Here, they were screened by the barrels, and wouldn't be spotted unless they stood, or someone looked right into the gap where they were hiding.

Several minutes went by. Kyle listened, but heard only the distant sounds of traffic and crickets. Then a mosquito came by, buzzing close to his ear. He held back swatting the thing, remaining perfectly motionless. In combat you learned never to give away your position, no matter what.

Glancing back at Erin, he saw her trying to swat it. She looked over and saw him watching her. She shrugged, rolled her eyes and stuck out her tongue. He had to look away not to laugh.

He could now hear the faint crunch of footsteps inching along the side of the building, getting closer. Seeing the shadow before the person, Kyle stuck out the shovel. The suspect tripped and Kyle jumped out, quickly pinning the man to the ground.

Suddenly a hard kick caught Kyle on the side. "Nice try," an unfamiliar woman's voice said.

Realizing he was fighting two people, he rolled away quickly and came up in a fighting stance.

The man jumped up and threw a right jab at him. Kyle blocked the punch and kicked at the man's groin. He missed his target and struck the man in the thigh, spinning him away.

The woman attacked from the side, swinging her foot around, trying to catch him in the gut.

He blocked the blow with his wrist, pain shooting up his arm.

Out of nowhere, he heard a loud, metallic thud, and the woman screamed, grabbing her knee. She collapsed to the ground as Erin brought the shovel back for another blow.

Kyle, crouched low, swung around to block an anticipated strike from the man, but the suspect had whirled around and was running away.

"That's Mike Bewley!" Erin yelled. "Go, I've got Frieda. If she tries to get up, I'll shovel her again."

Kyle handed her his backup pistol. "Screw the shovel. If she tries to get up, shoot her in the leg." He'd said it mostly to warn Frieda, but the look on Erin's face made him realize that she'd do just that if the woman moved.

Kyle raced after the suspect, knowing he'd be heading for the gate. When he got there, though, all he could see was the tail end of a car disappearing down the street.

He grabbed his phone and called it in to his brother. "Blue sedan, midsize, New Mexico tags too far away to read. That's all I've got. Erin's pretty sure it was Mike Bewley."

"I've got patrols in the area. Let's see if we can corner him."

"We'll need an ambulance, too," he said, jogging back to join Erin. "We caught Frieda Martinez, but Erin clocked her hard."

When he returned to the barrels, Erin was standing just out of Frieda's reach, pistol aimed at her. Frieda was still on her back, doubled up and groaning in pain.

As Kyle came up, she glared at him. "You attacked me for no reason, and she fractured my kneecap. I need to see a doctor. Are you going to just stand there like an idiot?"

"That all depends," Kyle said, not telling her help was already on its way. "I'm perfectly willing to wait until you tell me who you're working for and what you're after."

"I'm between jobs. I came here to look for Erin and saw two people sneaking around like thieves. I followed them, and got attacked. Now call an ambulance."

"We're not buying your story. What was Mike doing with you and why did you attack us?" Erin demanded.

"Mike who? I came here alone."

"Give it up, Frieda, or whoever you are," Kyle said. "You've been caught, and the charges are already piling up. Identity theft, terrorism, kidnapping, murder, attempted murder, assault—and that's just page one."

"Terrorism? That's a lot of bull. My name is Frieda Martinez and I'm an American citizen."

"Stop with the cover story. You're burned and you're not going anywhere," Kyle snapped. "We're going to find out everything, sooner or later. I guarantee it'll go easier on you if you cooperate."

He'd wait her out. Suspects generally hated long stretches of silence and would talk just to fill in the gap. It may have worked, too, but they soon heard the wail of sirens.

"I'm not talking till I get a lawyer. I know my rights," she said, grabbing her knee and moaning.

"Rights?" Kyle shook his head. "You're a terrorist, and the only chance you have to avoid a life sentence—or execution—is to spill your guts while you still can. Think about it."

KYLE STOOD WITH Preston as an officer climbed into the back of the ambulance next to Frieda.

"Don't worry. Perez is one of my best officers," Preston said. "Any chance Frieda will accept a deal and turn in the others?"

"That depends on who she really is, but there's always a chance, providing we make her a good enough offer. You might want to have a federal prosecutor on call for this one," Kyle said.

"You'll be coming in to question her?"

"Not right away. I'm going for a swim. I think Hank may have dropped those detonators in the river off the old highway bridge. Any idea where I can get some scuba gear?"

"Yeah, sure, the fire department has some they use for rescue operations. They'll loan it to the P.D. if I ask. You're guessing that Leland did that the night he came back?" Seeing Kyle nod, he added, "That river's cold, swift and pretty murky this time of year, you know."

"I've been trained for underwater recovery. Get the right gear, rope and a light. If it's there, I'll find it."

"Give me ten minutes to get things set up and I'll have one of our officers meet you at the bridge. Bill Walters is a former navy diver who works with the fire department on water-rescue situations. He can't dive for you right now, he broke a rib during one of our training ops, but he'll be able to guide you better than anyone else I know."

"Sounds good to me."

Kyle went to join Erin. "You doing okay?"

"Yeah, by now I'm getting used to surprises," she said, "but I'm starting to scare myself. I think I really would have shot Frieda if she'd tried to run."

"Had you told me you were ready to kill her, I would have worried, too, but you're talking about a nonlethal response. Why does that bother you?" he asked, leading her back to the SUV.

"I'm not a violent person. I don't even like to watch violent TV shows. Yet here I am accepting that the only way to communicate with these people is through violence."

"With terrorists, it's often all they understand."

"I can't accept that and still be me," she said. "The world needs warriors like you, but there's also a place for people like me."

"You'll go back to what's familiar to you soon, but until this is over and these people are behind bars, you'll have to keeping tapping into your warrior side."

He reached for her hand and gave it a gentle squeeze. "When I was growing up, I got through the tough times by reminding myself that life goes on and things change," he said. "Some of the foster homes I stayed in were great, others, not so much, but either way, I never stayed at one for long."

"Was it the foster parents who'd make or break it for you?"

"Not always. Sometimes I was the only Indian kid at the home, and when you're in the minority, problems often follow."

"So you've always been a warrior."

"Yeah, but I'm better trained now," he answered with a grin.

TWENTY MINUTES LATER Kyle turned off the old highway onto a dirt road, then came upon an open gate with a sign that read Conservancy Access Only. Passing through, he drove downhill into the bosque. Seeing a police SUV parked below and to the right of a concrete bridge pier, he continued on and parked to one side.

A uniformed officer stepped out of his department vehicle and Kyle went to meet him. "Officer Walters?"

"That's me. You ready to go for a swim?" the short, barrel-chested deputy asked.

"You bet," Kyle answered. "Show me what you've got."

Walters opened the back of the SUV and gestured inside. "Everything you need—except the wet suit might be a little tight. I'll attach a secure line to my vehicle and keep you from drifting during the search. The depth of the water here maxes out at about 10 feet this time of year, and the current is probably less than 2 mph, so you won't have to struggle to stay in one place," he said. "While you're below, I'll keep an eye on the witness."

"One minute." Kyle called Preston, took a quick photo of the officer and mailed it to him. "This is the guy, right?"

"That's him. You can trust Bill, he's one of our best."

"Anything new on Frieda yet?"

"She says she'll cooperate once the deal's in writing. What she wants is a guarantee that she won't be extradited, or sent to an overseas detention center. She also wants protection and a new identity," Preston said. "Since we're still trying to verify who she really is, we can't sign off on it yet."

Kyle went behind the SUV to put on the wet suit, which fit well except for the short length. Better than nothing, it would help retain his body heat and protect him from getting scraped by any drifting plant debris or submerged branches. After checking his equipment carefully, including a small but powerful LED lantern, he went to the river's edge and put on his fins.

"Stay with Officer Walters," he told Erin, and as he met Walters's gaze, saw him nod.

Kyle confirmed his intended search pattern and the emergency signal to haul him back to shore as he attached the line around his waist.

Ready, he stepped into cold water up to his knees, adjusted his mask and regulator, turned on the lamp, then eased forward into the river.

ERIN WATCHED KYLE disappear beneath the water, her heart beating overtime. Everything was so jumbled in her mind! She wanted this nightmare to end, but when it did, she'd lose Kyle.

What she'd felt when Frieda had attacked him, that overpowering need to protect him, had made her realize one thing. Kyle was her once-in-a-lifetime love. He was the soul mate her mother had told her about—her opposite who would complete her in every way that mattered.

Since Kyle willingly faced danger daily—a choice she found baffling—instinct assured her that he'd also need a counterpoint to that in his life. She wanted to be there for him and give him a place he could always retreat to and gather his strength.

As the minutes ticked by, she began to worry. Instinctively, she stepped closer to the water's edge.

"It's hard to see anything in that murky river," Walters said, as if reading her mind. "Visibility is probably five feet or less. I lost track of the glow from his lamp almost immediately. He'll have to work his way across to the opposite bank, and it's impossible to know what kind of junk might be down there in his way—car parts, cans, bottles and whatnot," he said. "But he's smart to begin with the downstream side. Even a dropped rock is carried by the current on its fall to the river bottom."

"He's convinced that what he's looking for is there, and he'll keep this up all night if he has to. No way he'll give up."

He smiled at her. "Good cops seldom do. It's not in our nature to back off or do a job halfway."

As she stared at the surface of the water, trying to spot the bubbles in the ripples of current or the glow from Kyle's lantern, she realized how much Kyle had changed her. She'd always seen herself as married to the land, but the truth was that would never be enough for her again. No matter what happened from now on, her heart belonged to him.

"Two quick tugs on the rope," the officer suddenly acknowledged. "He's coming back. I'll take up the slack and lead him in."

It wasn't long before Erin saw the glow of the light in the water, then Kyle's head appeared at the surface. As he approached the bank, she could see he was cradling a canvas bag in his arms. It was tied at the top.

Erin took hold of the rope as Officer Walters stepped to the river's edge and took the bag from Kyle's outstretched hands.

Kyle pulled back his mask and removed his mouthpiece. "Set it down gently, I don't want to crush the contents. There are concrete pavers in there, and if I'm right, electrical detonators that need to remain intact."

"Not pressure detonators?" Walters asked quickly, now holding the bag a little farther from his body as he stepped over to dry sand. "We can't set them off, right?"

Kyle laughed. "No, not unless you get struck by lightning. Set the bag down on the sand so I can open it up."

He brought out a sturdy diver's knife from the belt at his waist, then cut off the top of the canvas bag. Walters kneeled down beside him and held the fabric steady as Kyle continued to cut it away.

"Just what I expected," Kyle said. "Officer Walters, could you call my brother? Tell him I have what we needed and ask that he meet us at Daniel's office."

Glancing back at Erin as Walters stepped away, Kyle grinned. "Miss me?"

Erin smiled, then turned off the lantern and set it on the ground. "More than you know."

Surprised, he held her gaze a moment longer than usual. "Wait—what did *I* miss?"

He started to reach for her, then stopped, realizing he was dripping wet and wearing fins. "Duty calls. We'll pick this up later. Count on it."

Chapter Nineteen

"The detonators are the same make and model as the one you found in the box at Secure Construction. I've also got the cell-phone SIM card you recovered along with them buried in rice," Daniel said. "That'll dry it out and then we can see what made it so special that Leland wanted to make sure it was ruined."

"You really think you can restore it?" Kyle asked.

"No guarantees, but I've got a few tricks up my sleeve and some equipment that's nothing short of awesome," Daniel said. "As for the detonators, who knows if they still work? I certainly wouldn't want to try to use one of them now."

"I'm thinking Hank came home, saw the detonators, and not knowing when they'd come to claim them, decided to sink the lot on the way home," Kyle said. "If the terrorists showed up before we did, he could tell them the package hadn't arrived. Once he threw away the boxes in his office, who'd know otherwise?"

"I still don't understand how Frieda's connected to all this," Erin said.

"I've got the answer to that," Preston said, coming into the room.

"About time you got here," Kyle said with a quick half grin.

"While you were playing in the river, I was working," Preston shot back, barely able to keep a straight face. "Frieda's a Mexican national and her real name is Evelyn Santeiro. She does wet work for one of the Mexican cartels. The bartender at the Quarter Horse Bar, Ed Huff, found out who she really was, and offered her a chance to work for him as a mercenary. Huff, by the way, is an alias, too, but we haven't identified him yet."

"What's wet work?" Erin asked, confused.

"She was a hired assassin," Kyle answered.

Erin stared at him in shock.

"After her last hit—the competitor of the man she worked for—she was given forged papers and sent to the States to lay low," Preston said. "Then Evelyn met Huff, who, as it turned out, did some legitimate business with Mexican beer distributors. One of the salesmen recognized Evelyn and warned Huff to watch his back. Huff decided to use Evelyn's skills instead. He hooked her up with Bruce, so she'd have a family connection that would get her in close to Hank—Huff's objective. She didn't waste any time, and before long had Hank exactly where she wanted him."

"Poor Hank," Erin said.

"They were both manipulated, Hank *and* Bruce," Preston said. "The money Evelyn loaned Bruce came from Huff, and Evelyn thinks that Bruce is still under Huff's thumb. Bruce is being blackmailed and that money used as evidence to connect him to their operation and Hank's death."

"There are still some missing pieces to this puzzle," Kyle said, looking at Daniel. "I need to know what's on that SIM card."

"That's not something I can rush," Daniel said. "If I try to access it too soon, we risk losing everything that might still be on it. At least it wasn't crushed by those pavers."

Preston's phone rang and he answered. He mostly listened, then said, "I think that's an excellent idea, Mr. Leland. We'll be there shortly."

"What's going on?" Daniel asked.

"That was Bruce Leland, calling from his home. He told me that he's been searching for reasons his brother was killed, something that might also link up to Hank's work or presence in Spain. He checked on Google for the dates and discovered that there was a large jewel heist in Rota while Hank was there. Bruce thinks his brother may have been blackmailed into shipping the jewelry, mostly diamonds, to the U.S. He says that if this meshes with what we already suspect, we might consider going over to his mobile home and searching the place. His brother and he weren't on great terms, but Hank had a key."

"Hank didn't go to his brother's mobile home when he returned, and we already know what he shipped back wasn't jewels, but this is still a good opportunity to get a closer look at Bruce Leland," Kyle said. "It's possible that Hank mailed a third package also containing detonators to Bruce's place for safekeeping. If that's the case, Bruce may have opened the box and realized those would get him into a hell of a lot of trouble."

"So he calls us over, knowing we'll find them," Preston said.

"Yeah, and he can claim Hank put them there the night he returned. He has no idea I was tailing Hank and know exactly where he went," Kyle said.

"Not so fast, little brother. That's a bit of a reach," Daniel said. "Something about this has a real bad smell."

Kyle nodded. "I agree, and we'll need to watch each other's backs, but we still have to go check it out."

"Maybe you should leave Erin here," Daniel said.

"No way. I'm going," she said. "I may not like Bruce, but I know him better than any of you."

"Forget it, she comes," Kyle said. "Erin's under my protection."

Erin smiled. She sure did like the sound of that.

THEY DROVE TO Bruce's residence, Kyle leading the way, and Daniel with Preston in his police unit.

"The double-wide mobile home is beside the access road, which is next to a deep arroyo," Erin said, checking the Google map on the MDT screen. "There's also a lot of brush around the mobile home—at least when this photo was taken."

"No other buildings in the area?" Kyle asked, racing down the narrow highway.

"One shed at the far end of the property," she answered. As they made the turn onto the dirt road, Kyle noted two distinct sizes of tire tracks. "Looks like he's had visitors recently."

There was a loud boom from somewhere ahead, then two more. Kyle touched a button on the steering wheel and contacted Preston. "Gunfire!"

"I heard it," Preston said.

"Assume Bruce is under attack and go in hot," Daniel said.

"Come up and pass me, then keep going until you reach the residence," Kyle said. "I'll stop where the road is narrowest and use my vehicle to block the escape route. I'll advance on foot while you two give me some cover fire. Erin will stay behind the SUV. Preston, give me a situation report as soon as possible."

"Copy," Preston answered.

As Preston drove up behind them, Kyle inched over to the right. The deep arroyo's rim was now only a few feet outside Erin's door.

"You're close enough, Kyle. Any farther and we'll go over the edge," Erin said.

He nodded, slowing even more. Preston shot by a moment later.

"I just got a call from Leland," Preston said. "He says he's under attack. He's got a pistol and a thirty-thirty, but the two men firing at him have assault weapons of some kind. Leland's taken cover behind his pickup, and the men have taken firing positions behind their car."

They could hear the sound of rapid gunfire.

Ahead, Kyle saw Preston swerve to his left as he reached an open area. To the right, beside the ruins of an old wooden building, was a car. Two figures were hunched down behind it at opposite ends. One swung his weapon around and fired at Kyle's SUV. The bullet dinged off the front bumper.

"Hang on!" Kyle hit the brakes and slid to a stop, swerving at the last second so his vehicle was at a forty-five degree angle in the road. A big cloud of dust rose into the air. "Out my side," he told Erin, "and stay behind the vehicle."

As Erin slid down onto the ground, she handed Kyle his radio.

"Two shooters, beside the car," Kyle said, pistol in his right hand as he looked toward the scene.

"Bruce's pickup isn't even close to his house. Why would he park in that location unless he planned to ambush someone coming in?" Preston pointed out.

"Looks like Bruce set these guys up," Kyle said.

"Problem is, they have more firepower than we do, so we need a new tactical plan," Preston said. "I've called for backup, but it'll be at least ten minutes before they can get here."

"Okay, here's what we do," Kyle said. "I'll grab the assault rifle and come up in line with the arroyo, cutting off their retreat. Once I've distracted them, Preston, you can circle around behind the mobile home and flank them. Daniel, you provide cover fire."

"How soon?" Daniel's voice came over the speaker.

"On my mark." Kyle reached into the SUV and brought out the assault rifle from beneath the seat.

"What about me?" Erin asked.

Kyle handed her his pistol. "Take it, just in case, but I want you to stay here, behind the SUV. If they get close, jump in, shut the door and hunker down. You can listen in using the vehicle's radio. I'll keep the connection open."

"I'd rather go with you."

"It's too risky. You'll be safe, I won't let them get close to you, darlin'."

"Thanks for sharing, Kyle." Preston's voice came over the radio. "Now, can we get on with it? I'm about to doze off."

"Yeah, okay, moving out now. Cover me."

Kyle circled around the back of the SUV and for the first time saw how close he'd come to the edge. He had to inch sideways down the passenger side. The embankment to his right was too steep to walk along without risking a slide to the bottom in the loose sand and gravel.

Once at the front bumper, he gave his brothers a quick wave. Daniel started shooting, aiming high to keep their attackers pinned while Preston raced toward the house.

Kyle ran forward, zigzagging and crouched low, his assault rifle up and ready. One of the suspects saw him just then and began firing. Bullets whistled by him, then one struck the receiver of his rifle, knocking it out of his hand. The weapon fell to the ground precariously close to the ledge of the arroyo.

Kyle flattened and reached out to recover it, but had to roll away as slugs dug into the ground right around the fallen weapon.

He looked over at Daniel, who was changing magazines, unaware of what was going on.

"Kyle!" Erin ran toward him, firing her pistol at the car as she moved.

"Erin, get down!" Leaping forward, he grabbed the assault rifle and rolled. Groping for the pistol grip while bringing the weapon against his body, he cut his fingers on the edge of the trigger guard. It had been ripped loose and twisted around by a bullet strike, the same hit that had broken off the trigger. The weapon was damaged, useless now except as a club.

Cursing the lucky hit, he looked up and saw Erin down on one knee, shooting, one round at a time, at something behind him.

He glanced back. The shooters were now in their car, racing straight toward him. Scrambling to his feet as the vehicle bore down on him, he lunged toward the opposite side of the road, diving into a tuck and roll, feeling the rush of air as the car brushed by.

He sprang to his feet and spun around to look. Erin, still on one knee, fired two more shots at the car. It angled to the left, heading right at her.

"Jump!" he yelled, knowing it was her only chance.

She dropped and slid headfirst over the embankment just in time. The car cut right again, accelerated and raced down the road, barely squeezing by his SUV.

Kyle raced to the edge of the arroyo. He'd never

had anyone outside his family step out into the open in the middle of a gunfight and risk everything to save him.

"A little help?" she called out.

Shaken, he looked down and found her about five feet down the embankment, struggling to climb back up.

"I've got you." He flattened, reached down, grabbed her by both wrists, then pulled her up to the road.

"How could you have done something so crazy!" he demanded, pulling her all the way to her feet. "You were supposed to stay behind the car. You could have been killed!" He gripped her by the shoulders and gave her a little shake.

"Kyle, you needed my help," she said firmly, holding his gaze and refusing to back down. "You would have done the same for me—and not just 'cause you're NCIS."

Her words broke him. Putting all the emotions raging inside him into it—fear, possessiveness, protectiveness—he kissed her hard.

When he finally stopped to take a breath, his body was rock hard.

"Save it, Romeo," Preston's voice came over the radio that had ended up on the sandy earth. "In case you haven't noticed, the bad guys are getting away."

"This isn't over," Kyle whispered in her ear.

"We'll settle things later." Not giving her a chance to ask what he meant, he took her hand and raced down the road to where his brothers were questioning Bruce.

Bruce's gaze shifted to Erin as they came up. "*You* again! You're part of this, aren't you?"

"Still trying to point the finger at someone else, huh, Bruce?" Kyle said. "Won't work, we already know the truth. You set this little gunfight up, but it almost got you killed, didn't it?"

"What the hell are you talking about? I called you here to search my house. Those guys showed up before you did and I had to defend myself. They were demanding that I give them the detonators or they'd kill me. I had no idea what they were talking about. What detonators? I thought this was about stolen gems," he said, rubbing the back of his neck.

"Nice try, but your story's full of bull. What really happened?" Kyle said, his voice flat and menacing.

"Dude, you still don't you get it, do you? These guys are real, actual terrorists, not just gun-happy nut jobs. When I told them I didn't know about any detonators, they pulled out pistols and threatened to kill me. I told them yeah, okay, the stuff's in my pickup. When I reached in and brought out my thirty-thirty, they ran back to their car. I thought they'd take off, but once they whipped out those assault rifles, I knew I was screwed. If you people hadn't shown up when you did, I'd be dead."

"So you got a good look at these two men. Did you recognize either of them?" Daniel said.

"No, but they seemed to know a lot about me. Go ahead and search the place all you want. I'm not spending another night here. I'm going to move into my brother's house."

"You're not going anywhere, not until we're finished with you," Preston snapped.

Bruce rolled his left shoulder as if working the kinks out, then froze and sucked in his breath. "Ow!" Moving carefully, he reached up with his right hand. When he brought it back down, his fingertips were bloody. "Holy crap! I've been shot!"

Daniel came up just as Bruce opened his shirt and pushed it away from his shoulder.

"The bullet just grazed you, guy. I've seen worse rope burns. You're fine, just wash up and put some disinfectant on it," he said.

"Dude, I'm *bleeding!*"

"Man up, will ya?" Preston said, staring at Bruce with barely hidden contempt.

"I need medical attention right now! I need an ambulance."

The brothers looked at each other and Kyle rolled his eyes. "Okay, fine. You can go to an urgent care and get the injury cleaned and bandaged up," he said, nodding to Preston.

"I'll have a patrol officer take Mr. Leland to be treated. No way I can justify calling an ambulance," Preston said.

Leaving Daniel to guard Bruce, Preston, Kyle and Erin went inside the house, which was unlocked.

"My gut's telling me that Bruce has been working with these people all along, maybe not even knowing who they were and what they were really doing until they killed his brother," Kyle said.

"He's thinking he's next, and that's why he turned on them," Preston answered.

They searched the mobile home until they heard the patrol car pulling up. Stepping back outside, they watched as Bruce was loaded into the unit.

Preston hurried to speak to the officer, then met with Daniel. "The officer will have to go back on patrol once he delivers Leland to the urgent care center. Until I can assign a detective to keep him under surveillance 24/7, will you stick with him?"

"You've got it," Dan said, then walked over to the squad car.

Preston rejoined Kyle and Erin, who were still outside the mobile home. "We may not have been able to identify these two gunmen, but we do know we've got at least three suspects running around."

"Ed Huff, Mike Bewley and Ron Mora," Kyle said with a nod. "I think that Huff is their leader, the one who organized the cell and recruited most of the others."

"They're still looking for the detonators, so that's going to put you two in the crosshairs," Preston said.

"By a process of elimination, I'm sure they're now convinced I'm the one who has them," Erin said.

"The best advice I can give you two is to stay on the move," Preston said.

"That's what I intend to do. You know where to find us," Kyle said, leading Erin back to the SUV.

"We're just going to drive around?" she asked.

"No. There's something I need to pick up first, then afterward we need to prepare. They're going to throw everything they have at us," he said. "Things have been rough so far, but they're about to get a whole lot tougher."

Chapter Twenty

Kyle drove directly to Hartley's downtown district, his gaze continually darting to his rearview mirror.

"I know you're figuring out our next move, so I haven't interrupted you, but it's been twenty minutes and I'd really like to know where we're going," Erin said.

"We're here," Kyle answered, parking in front of a small store off Main Street called Southwest Treasures. "A good friend of Hosteen Silver's, Pablo Ortiz, owns the place. He hand carved the fetishes that were given to my brothers and me."

She sat up, excited. "Am I going to get a fetish?"

"Yes. I've finally figured out the right match for you. Receiving a fetish is a family tradition for us and now you'll be part of that." He reached for her hand and held her gaze. "You matter to me, Erin."

He saw it in her eyes. She'd wanted to hear him say that he loved her, but those words didn't come easily. He'd never spoken them to anyone before.

Before she could answer him, a short, rotund man came out and met them by the car.

"So, you gonna sit out here forever?" he said.

"Pablo, it's good to see you," Kyle said, laughing as he climbed down out of the SUV.

Once they were inside his shop, Erin, as if sensing the two men wanted to talk privately, walked off to look at an exhibit of pueblo pottery.

"So what brings you here today?" Pablo asked Kyle.

"I need a special fetish—Black Bear."

He gave Kyle a long look. "There are many kinds of bear fetishes. Some are for hunting, others have different uses. What are your plans for it?"

"What Fox is to me, Black Bear will be to her," he said, his voice quiet.

Pablo watched Erin as she strolled slowly around the shop, looking at the merchandise. "You want a bear fetish that will give her courage in times of trouble, and strength in the face of changes."

He nodded, not surprised by Pablo Ortiz's insight. "Yes."

Pablo considered for a while before replying. "I have one I finished carving yesterday. Something told me it would be needed."

"May I see it, uncle?" he asked, using the term out of respect.

"I'll bring it out to you," he said. "Although I usually use jet to carve Black Bear, this one's made from black marble. I started it a while back, and even as I worked on it, I knew its destiny was set," he said going through the door leading to his workroom.

A minute later Pablo returned. The inch-and-a-half-long carving depicted Bear standing on its hind legs as if surveying the area. Its marble surface gleamed in the light. The fetish was carved with painstaking attention to detail. Each of Bear's paws, held high, showed extended claws, yet its muzzle was in a relaxed position. "It depicts power in stillness, and the wisdom to discern an enemy from a friend."

"I'll take it, uncle. It's perfect," Kyle said.

"I'll place it in a *jish*," he said, referring to a medicine bag with pollen inside.

"Thank you."

Erin came over after Pablo left to get the fetish ready. "He carries so many beautiful and interesting things here," she said, gesturing to a display cabinet across the room. "The fetishes are over there behind the glass."

"Those aren't for you. What I have in mind has to be a special carving."

Her eyes lit up and she smiled. "Did you have to order it, or is he getting it right now?"

"He'll bring it out, but you'll have to wait a little longer to see it. There's a place we need to go first. It's my way of honoring the tradition Hosteen

Silver began when he gave my brothers and me our own fetishes."

"Tradition," she said, and nodded thoughtfully. "I should get something for you, too. You've spoken about balance before." She looked around quickly.

"You've given me more than I ever had a right to expect," he said softly.

As Pablo returned with the pouch, he smiled at Erin, then at Kyle. "You've chosen well, nephew," he said.

Once they were on the road again, she shifted in her seat. "Was Pablo talking about the fetish you chose for me, or about us?"

"I'm not sure," he said. "Sometimes it's better not to ask. In a lot of ways he's like Hosteen Silver. His predictions are amazingly accurate. Whether that's because he's a good detective, or the result of a gift that goes beyond our ability to understand, I can't say."

They were soon heading northeast. Part of the trip was over dirt roads, and after a long, bumpy, teeth-jarring drive, they arrived at a spot where the river was fed by a large creek.

"This is it," he said.

"Where are we?" she asked, getting out of the SUV.

"It's a sacred place. The *Diné,* the Navajo people, come here to pray for success in war."

He led the way to the water's edge, near the junction of the two streams, then lifted out his pollen-covered fetish from its pouch. Next, he took the one that would become hers and dipped them both in the water. Afterward, he covered each with pollen once again, put Fox back in his *jish,* and placed Bear in her extended hand.

"The waters here have power. Using the fetish, we made an offering of pollen, and asked for a blessing in return, that our fetishes be made strong, so they can strengthen us. It'll bring us both luck and skill in the fight ahead."

She looked at the small bear carving in her hand, turning it over in her fingers. "It's beautiful."

"Bear will become your spiritual sister—if you allow her to be. She'll bring you confidence and courage in times of trouble," he said. "Should we need to pull away from a situation, or fall back, Bear will also be there to remind you that withdrawal is a way to gather strength. Hibernation is part of nature's pattern, too.

"Erin, I've spent my life taking chances, but there was one risk I never would take—letting anyone get close to me. Then you came into my life," he said, drawing her into his arms. "I'm going to fight to keep you after this is over."

"Will I be exciting enough for you in the long run?"

"I love you. I've never said that to anyone in

my life, but it's how I feel. All you have to do is love me back."

She drew in a breath. "I do," she whispered as he leaned down and kissed her.

He was gentle this time, coaxing but not demanding. She'd seen the hardened warrior, but now he was patient and tender.

After a moment he eased his hold. "There's something I need you to think about. No matter what work I choose after I come home, being an investigator will be at the heart of it. It's what I do best. Will you be able to handle the stress that comes with my job, of knowing that one day something could happen and I may not come home?"

She didn't answer right away. "I don't know."

"Think hard about it, and when you're ready, we'll talk again."

He took her hand as they moved to a narrow channel in the stream where the water was very still. "Do you see it?" he asked, pointing down. Although the river's current was rapid not twenty feet away, two leaves had found each other in a point of stillness. "Together they form a heart."

"Maybe it's a sign," she said and smiled. As she watched, the leaves swirled gently but continued to stay together.

The peace of that wonderful moment vanished instantly the second Kyle's phone rang. He looked down at the caller ID and his expression instantly changed back to agent mode.

"Time to get to work," he told her.

In the SUV heading back to Hartley, Kyle continued his conversation with Preston.

"We questioned Bruce Leland," Preston said, "but I couldn't hold him. He lawyered up and insisted he was the vic in what happened. He'd been loaned some money, and that was being used to try to link him to his brother's death. Blackmail, he called it. I didn't expect to hear from him again anytime soon, but he just called. He said that he figured out where his brother hid the detonators and wanted to meet at Secure Construction. I tried to get him to give me the location, but he refused. He said someone might be listening in. He also insisted that Erin be there, that she's the only person who would be able to figure out the combination to the electronic lock."

"Do you know what he's talking about?" Kyle asked her.

"No. Hank installed one electronic lock on the door to the secure room, but that was for demonstration purposes only. I know how it works, and have operated it when showing the design to clients, but that's about it. I don't know of any other locks like that on the property."

"After last time, I don't trust him," Preston said.

"I'll meet you there and get some patrol units in place, too."

"Hang back. Let him think Erin and I showed up alone. You can monitor what's being said through my cell phone. I'll keep it on speaker in my shirt pocket," Kyle said.

"All right. If Bruce is up to something again, stall and give us a chance to move in," Preston said. "Paul will stick by the computer and track your GPS location, and Gene's already in town, ready to move. We'll have all the manpower we need."

"Just in case we get separated, Erin's carrying a tracking device," Kyle said, giving him the access codes to monitor it.

"It's secure?"

"I have it in a small pouch I'm wearing around my neck," she said. "But just in case they search me, I'm going to put the pouch in my bra. It'll stay put."

Preston didn't comment, and Kyle smiled.

"One more thing. I heard from Daniel. He was able to recover enough from that SIM card to verify that they were blackmailing Hank. He retrieved copies of some of the documents they sent him while he was in Spain. They'd hacked into his construction records, altered entries and made it look like he was making phony purchases and overcharging the DOD."

"How were they able to hack into our system?"

Erin asked, surprised. "Hank was really careful about things like that."

"My guess is that Frieda—Evelyn Santeiro—managed to get Hank's passwords. She's still holding out, but she's intimated as much."

"No one's really safe from these people," Erin said, and shuddered.

"Don't worry. I have your back, and my brothers will have mine. You're in good hands."

They arrived at Secure Construction twenty minutes later. Kyle glanced over at her, a somber expression on his face. "Get ready. A van's been tailing us for the past five minutes, and now it's show time."

Chapter Twenty-One

Kyle slowed down and stopped at the curb just before the turn leading to the gates, which were closed. "I have the key. Should I get out and open them?" Erin asked.

"No. Sit tight," he said, watching a white van approach from behind.

As it passed by, Kyle saw Bruce at the wheel. The van pulled up to the curb, and parked in front of them. "Come out on my side and stay behind me," Kyle said, exiting as Bruce stepped out into the street.

Bruce took a few steps toward them, then the side door opened and a man wearing a ski mask jumped down, his gun aimed at Kyle.

Kyle moved in front of Erin. "Bruce, you're playing for the team that murdered your brother?"

"No, and this isn't my fault!" he said, looking back and forth between Kyle and the man with the gun.

"Shut up," the man said, motioning with his

pistol barrel for Bruce to walk back toward them. Another gunman slipped out the side door, and a third came around from the passenger's side of the van. All were masked and kept their weapons pointed at Kyle and Erin.

"I never saw them coming, I swear," Bruce said.

The first armed man came within ten feet of Kyle. "Put your weapons on the ground—and do it slowly."

"Okay, Ed," Kyle said, recognizing the voice of Ed Huff, the bartender at the Quarter Horse Bar.

"I knew you'd recognize me," Huff said.

"We've known you were involved for some time, so why the masks?" Kyle asked, removing the pistol from his holster and ejecting the magazine before placing the weapon down on the pavement.

"Just a precaution in case something went wrong," Huff replied.

"Mike Bewley, even with that dumb mask, I know you just by your posture," Erin said, looking closely at one of the other two. "The police already know you and Huff are involved. Why are you making it worse for yourself?"

"Shut up," Mike said.

"Now get rid of *your* weapons," Huff ordered, pointing his .45 pistol at Erin.

"I haven't got any," she answered as the third man moved up to frisk Kyle.

"He's clean."

"Ron Mora. You're not fooling anyone, either," Erin said, as he came over to frisk her, too.

"We already know who you are, and so do the police," Kyle pointed out, glad to know Preston was listening in.

"Yeah, good point. This mask is bugging me, and if someone drives by and sees us they'll be on their cell phone in a nanosecond," Mike said, yanking his off.

Ron Mora pulled his off, too, even as Huff cursed and took off his own.

Kyle knew that he had to draw things out until either he or Preston could make a move. Huff probably killed Moe, and he'd kill again unless he was stopped. "Huff, you're working with some half-assed ecoterrorist clowns and your mission's been compromised. We know what your target is, and security has already been doubled. Your best chance is to give yourself up."

"Shut up. I'm in charge here," Huff said, then added, "Take your boots off."

Kyle did as he was told, and Huff saw the backup pistol in the attached holster on Kyle's ankle. "Use your left hand, finger and thumb, and place that down on the ground—gently," he snapped.

Kyle did, then put his boots back on.

Huff gestured with his .45, glancing up and

down the empty street. "You three move onto the sidewalk behind the van so we can't be seen."

After they'd done as he'd ordered, Huff stared at Erin. "Give me the detonators right now or I'll shoot your boyfriend in the gut and let him bleed to death," he said. "I'm out of patience."

"Erin, give them whatever they want," Bruce said, his voice rising in fear.

Huff pulled back the hammer on his pistol. "Your choice, lady."

"No, wait!" Erin screamed. "You're right. I know where they are, but if you shoot any of us, I'll die before I hand them over."

"So you had them all along!" Bruce said, surprised. "You lied to me, to us!" he added, glancing at Kyle.

"Yeah. Forgive me, Kyle, Bruce. I found them by mistake and believed that as long as they stayed hidden, no one else would die."

Kyle glared at Erin, feigning anger, though he knew she was also doing her best to stall.

"Where are they?" Huff demanded.

Erin was shaking now. "Hank put them in a padded envelope and told me to hide them. He knew you guys were coming. After you killed him, I knew they weren't safe here anymore, so I moved them."

"Where?" Huff growled. "I'm through playing games."

"The police were searching this place inch by inch, so I sneaked the envelope into my tote and buried it later where no one would ever think of searching. It's way out in the desert, and if you want those detonators, we'll have to drive there."

Huff shook his head. "I don't buy it. You're stalling, hoping for a miracle that'll save your sorry butts. Prove that you've seen those detonators. Describe them."

Kyle felt his blood turn to ice. The only closeup photo she'd seen of them had been on Daniel's computer. If her description was off...

"I've seen detonators before, but these were different from the ones I'm familiar with," she said. "They were metal, painted light brown and labeled in Spanish, which makes sense because that's where they came from. They were about three inches long, and had, let's see, red and green wires. They were the electric kind. There were at least eight or nine of them, maybe ten. I was too nervous to count them."

Kyle almost smiled. He couldn't have given a better description himself. Her memory was perfect. Unfortunately, all the detonators were now inside a secure evidence bunker, way out of their reach.

"Yeah, okay," Huff said. "Take us to where they are."

"Damn," Kyle spat out, thinking fast. "You hid

them when I took you to my foster father's ranch, didn't you?"

Erin hung her head, trying to look embarrassed, and nodded.

"Yeah, I buried them beside some rocks."

Huff stepped closer and aimed the barrel of his gun at Kyle's head. "I want precise directions—down to the inch."

"I can't do that. It's not like there are street signs out there, and all the rocks look pretty much the same. The best I can do is try to retrace my steps. I'll recognize it when I see it."

"If you're playing me, I'll shoot all three of you and leave you in the desert to die slowly," Huff growled.

"You don't think I know that?" Gulping in a breath, she added in a trembling voice, "I'll take you there, but before I do I need a guarantee that you'll let us go after you get what you want."

"Maybe I should put it in writing?" Huff said, mocking her.

Kyle stayed rock still, watching. *Careful, Erin. Don't push them too hard.*

"Once we've hiked up the trail about a third of the way, I want you to let Bruce go. Out in the middle of nowhere is fine. I've never liked him anyway. It'll take him hours to get back to civilization or find help, so he won't be a threat to you," she said, and saw Huff nod. "Next, you have to let Kyle go. After they're both free, I'll lead you to the exact spot."

"Deal. But if either man causes any trouble, I'll kill both of them. You're the only one I need alive. One more thing. Before we go, hand over your cell phones."

Kyle slipped his phone out of his shirt pocket. As he did, he touched the display and shut it down, making sure no one knew Preston had been monitoring their face-off.

"Toss it over," Huff ordered.

Kyle did as he asked.

Ron stomped on it with his boot, then put it on the ground in front of the van's left front tire.

"Good idea. Once we leave, it'll be extra crunchy," Mike said. "Where's your phone, Erin?"

"The police took it away. We've relied on Kyle's."

"Then you won't mind if we pat you down."

"Do I have a choice?"

"No," Huff said, nodding to Mike.

Kyle clenched his jaw as Mike ran his hands over Erin slowly, deliberately baiting him. To her credit, Erin never even flinched.

"No phone," Mike said at last.

Huff gestured toward the van. "Okay, let's go. Bruce, Kyle, get into the van and lie face down on the floor. Don't roll over or turn around to look. You'll have two guns aimed at your backs, so don't go stupid on me," he warned. "Erin, you're riding up front with me. If you make one wrong move, the men will pay the price."

AFTER AN HOUR and a half on the road, Erin led them onto a sturdy one-lane wooden bridge that crossed a deep arroyo. They drove across slowly, the tires rumbling on the rough timbers below.

Up ahead there was a fork in the road. "I remember those rough sandstone walls. That bluff is familiar, too, but I was only out here once. From this direction, I'm not sure whether to go left or right to find the trail that leads into the canyon."

"Try harder, or we'll be one passenger short," Huff ordered.

She pointed to the east road, then hesitated, and shook her head. "Get Kyle up here, he knows the way, at least to the house. I can find it from there."

"If this is a trick—" Huff growled.

"Guy, look around you! There are no street signs, just sand, mesas, sagebrush and piñon trees. You're going to tell me that the view to your left looks that much different than the one on your right?"

Huff stopped the van and ordered Mike to bring Kyle up front. "Erin, in the middle. Kyle, sit by the passenger's door. Mike, stay in the back but keep your gun trained on Kyle. If he tries to jump out, kill him."

"Okay, where do we go?" Huff asked once they were all seated again.

"Take the right. You'll find some recent vehicle tracks there that'll lead you to the house," Kyle said. "Once we get there, you'll have to park the van and hike the rest of the way."

Kyle studied the look on Huff's face. As soon as they were of no further use, Bruce, Erin and he would be dead. He'd have to help Erin stall until his brothers got into place. From the fresh tracks, he knew help was already there—somewhere.

THEY WERE ON foot now, more than a mile from the van, having left it beside the ranch house. Mike was several feet behind Kyle, weapon aimed at his back as they hiked across uneven ground dotted with sandstone outcrops and tough sagebrush. Erin hadn't said anything since they'd passed the empty sheep pens, and from her gait, Kyle could tell she was already exhausted.

"Everything looks the same out here this late in the afternoon," Erin said, stopping and looking toward the rugged sandstone bluff to the south. "I'm having trouble finding the spot again. I remember going past a gap in the cliffs, but I'm not sure I'm heading in the right direction."

"Figure it out," Huff snapped. "Your lives depend on it."

Ten minutes later, they were hiking among

waist-high boulders that, over the centuries, had tumbled down from the cliffs. Huff was breathing hard, and so were Ron and Bewley. To Kyle's surprise, Erin actually seemed stronger than before.

"You should have let Bruce go a half hour ago," Erin said, stopping. "We had a deal, Huff."

"New terms. I'll let you all go after I get what I want."

"No. Once you have the detonators, you'll kill us. Either honor your deal, or this is as far as we all go."

"Even if I let Bruce and Kyle go, what makes you think I won't kill *you* after I get what I want?"

"Because there'll be two people who will know what happened," she answered. "I'm betting that one, or both, will eventually make it out of the canyon."

"You're looking at this all wrong. Once I have the detonators, I'll have no need to kill any of you. Nature will take care of it for me. My men and I will tie you up, return to the van, burn down the house, then drive away. It'll take you hours to get loose, then two or three days to hike out of here, if wild animals or the icy nights don't get you first. I'm willing to let fate decide whether you live or die. Either way, by the time you manage to reach a phone, or flag down help, we'll be halfway across the country."

"And if I refuse to take you to the detonators?"

"Bang, bang, bang. You'll all be dead," Huff replied, pointing his gun back and forth. "And we'll still get away."

"Take the deal, Erin. It'll give us a fighting chance," Kyle said.

"Good advice. Listen to the man," Huff added.

They inched along for another hundred yards, walking parallel to a high bluff, when Huff's patience finally ran out.

"Okay, I've had it. No more stalling or one of you dies right now," Huff said, drawing his pistol again.

"Relax," Kyle snapped, pointing three hundred yards away. "The gap in the cliff she talked about is just past the next arroyo." With luck, his brothers would be in position by now.

"Okay, if that's where you said you buried the detonators, Erin," Huff said, "where, exactly, are they?"

"You hid them at the place I showed you, didn't you, where I played as a kid?" Kyle asked, hoping she'd pick up on his cue. "In the metal box I'd buried my old keepsakes in, too, I'll bet."

She nodded, trusting him. "It was big enough and still looked watertight and solid. I knew that eventually you'd find them."

Kyle wanted to kiss her. Once they set out in that direction, Preston, Daniel and Gene would know exactly where they were headed. Paul, monitoring the tracker, would know it, too.

"I'll take you up the easiest trail. Let's get this over with," Kyle said.

Each of Hosteen Silver's sons had staked out their own special places in Copper Canyon. As foster kids who weren't used to trusting anyone, one of the first things they'd all done was find a secure hiding spot for the things they'd treasured most.

He'd found out years later that each of them, including Hosteen Silver, had known where he'd hidden his small stash, but no one had ever disturbed it, respecting his privacy.

That had been years ago, and he'd never come back for the box. Undoubtedly it was still there. If not, their time would run out then.

After walking another fifteen minutes up the sandy bottom of the arroyo, they climbed out next to the cliff and entered a narrow, steep-sided canyon visible only up close. From this point on, Kyle knew there was a chance that Erin's tracking signal would be lost.

Only two people could walk side by side down the trail, which climbed gently at first, then more steeply. The going was slow, but they soon arrived at a small grotto cut into the base of the rock wall. He gave Erin a tiny nod.

"It's over there," Erin said, waving at an indeterminate point ahead. "I don't know the exact spot, because it was almost dark by the time I got here. I packed down the dirt again with my shoes, but the wind and rain have worn away the tracks. You'll have to dig."

"You," Huff said, gesturing to Kyle. "Get busy."

He almost smiled. *Great save, Erin!* "All right, but I'm going to need a shovel."

"You see a shovel anywhere? Make do."

"Without a shovel, I may be digging for an hour," Kyle warned. "At least give me a knife with a long enough blade."

"That's not going to happen. Start now or someone's going to bleed," Huff snarled.

As Kyle began digging with his hands, Huff pushed Erin forward. "Help him out."

After digging about a foot into the sand, they found nothing.

Huff glared at Erin. "If you're playing a game—"

"No, I swear I'm not," she said. "If I could try poking through the dirt…"

"Find her a stick," Huff ordered Bewley. "No longer than a foot, though."

A few minutes later, Bewley returned with a juniper branch as big around as his wrist and the length of a ruler.

She dug away more dirt, then poked through the sand layer.

"Maybe you should move a little more to your left," Kyle said. "The sand looks softer there so that's probably where you loosened it up."

Erin swept more dirt aside, then poked the branch downward. "I've got it," she said, thumping against something hard.

As the men focused on Erin's find, Kyle felt a trickle of dirt drop down onto his neck. He looked over at Erin, scooped up a handful of dirt, and nodded almost imperceptibly, signaling for her to do the same.

Erin scooped up more sand, and as Huff bent down to see what she'd uncovered, she threw the dirt into his face.

Kyle tossed a handful at Ron, then jabbed him in the stomach with the stick. Ron recovered quickly, but as he raised his pistol a figure dropped from above, knocking him to the ground. It was Preston.

Huff, still spitting dirt, fired blindly, the bullet ricocheting off the rock wall. Kyle kicked the weapon out of his hand and Huff yelped as the bone in his trigger finger snapped.

A second later, Gene dropped down, pinning Huff to the ground with an elbow to his neck.

Mike tried to maneuver around the chaos in the cramped space and get a clear shot, but Daniel came up right behind him. "Drop the gun, or I'll drop you," he growled, jamming the barrel of his weapon into the man's back.

Moments later, all three terrorists were face down on the ground, lining the narrow path. Preston and Gene stood on either side of them, weapons out.

Erin had Huff's pistol, but her hands were shaking so badly she quickly handed Kyle the gun. "You take it. I'm shaking like a leaf and I'm going to end up squeezing the trigger by accident."

Kyle put his arm around her. "You did great. You read my signals like a pro."

"Hey, what about my flying-cop routine?" Preston said, handcuffing the men as Gene kept them covered. "Remember when we used to ambush each other like that?"

"Who knew the good ole days playing Indians and Indians would serve us so well in the bad new days," Daniel said, grinning.

Kyle's brothers got the men on their feet, including Bruce, and led them back up the path toward the canyon opening.

Erin sat down, her back against the rock face. "I need a minute," she said. "My heart's still beating so loud you can hear the echo."

"It's okay, darling. It's over," he said, sitting next to her. "Just in time for the chile harvest, too."

She laughed. "*Now* you're interested in growing and picking chile?"

"What New Mexican doesn't look forward to the scent of roasting chiles? I know where we can plant a field or two, if and when you decide to leave Secure Construction, that is. Suppose you can do both?"

She leaned into him and he put his arm around her, drawing her even closer to his side.

She remained quiet for a while, snuggling against him. "How can you stay in a job where you have to face life and death situations like these? I've never been so scared in my life!"

"The danger is what initially drew me to the job. I didn't want to let anyone get close to me, and living on the edge almost guaranteed that."

"And now?"

"I'm finally ready to come home, to stop running." Lifting two badly corroded snaps, he opened the box she'd uncovered. There was a faded five dollar bill inside and an empty metal key ring. He took it out and held it for a moment.

"The key ring belonged to my dad. The house key it held had to be returned to our landlord, but I was allowed to keep this. It wasn't worth anything to anyone, except me," he said. "For a long time, I pretended that it was magic and would somehow lead dad back to me. After the mine collapsed, his body was never recovered, so I kept hoping…"

"I'm so sorry," she said, taking his hand and lacing her fingers through his.

"That was the dream of a boy. Now I have another dream." He pressed the key ring into her palm. "I wish I had a better ring to give you but, for now, this is the only one I've got. I'll be coming home for good soon. Will you be there for me? Can you accept the uncertainty that comes with the work I do?"

"You're a warrior, Kyle, and your work is all part of who you are—the man I love," she said softly. "When you get back, I'll be waiting."

He kissed her, then offered her a hand up. As they walked out of the canyon, they saw the three prisoners sitting on the ground, their backs to the mesa wall. Gene and Daniel were guarding them.

Preston greeted them. "A couple of four-wheel-drive vehicles are on their way up. One is for the prisoners and Bruce Leland. The feds will have to decide what charges, if any, will be brought against Hank's brother. The other SUV will take you back to Hartley. You're needed there now."

"You're going to want our statements," Kyle said with a nod.

"Yeah, that, and your boss will want to debrief you. He flew into Hartley and is at the station. He told me that Ed Huff is really Eduardo Cruz, a college dropout who spent several years in Spain and is connected to Invierno Nuclear—nuclear winter—an obscure anti-nuke group. The two men who were killed the day of the kidnapping attempt are Spanish nationals with radical ties. You'll have to fill him in on the locals that Cruz recruited."

"We're lucky he stayed away for as long as he did. He's not a patient man."

"Do you think he'll try to make it difficult for you to leave your job with NCIS?" Erin asked.

"Probably, but home is where I choose to be now, and nothing's going to keep me away."

Chapter Twenty-Two

It was to be a farewell party for Kyle, though he'd be home to stay in a month or so, and by unanimous vote, the brothers had decided to hold it at the ranch house in Copper Canyon.

"What's bothering you?" Erin, riding beside him in the rental pickup, asked at last. "You've been so quiet since we left Secure Construction."

"Today, I'm going to open the letter that Hosteen Silver left for me just before he died," he said. "It's time."

"A private note, not his journal?"

"The journal was a record of his thoughts, but in addition to that, he left each of us a letter. Judging from the ones my brothers received, they all contain a prediction of some kind. Of course they're worded in a way that only makes sense after the fact. It was his way."

"I would have opened mine immediately," she said. "How did you keep your curiosity from getting the best of you?"

"Some of my brothers couldn't wait, either, but after they read theirs, things happened that eventually led them up the aisle. They're happily married, but I was gun-shy, so I figured I'd wait a decade or two for mine," he said, and laughed. "Now that marriage is in the cards for me, I figure I'm ready to read his letter," he said, tapping his index finger on the wheel restlessly.

"Yet you're still worried," she said. "Why?"

He took a moment before answering. "All my brothers, with the exception of Rick, who's still out of the country, read theirs before meeting their future wives. It's easier to make things fit in when you go from that perspective, but I've already found my match. What if after reading the letter, we all realize that his predictions weren't real, that in fact, we made them self-fulfilling prophecies?"

"You're worried that his prediction won't make sense in light of what's already happened between us?" Seeing him nod, she continued. "You hold Hosteen Silver in high regard, and that's the way it should be, but no one's right one hundred percent of the time. The problem isn't what's in the letter, it's with your expectations."

"Good point," he said, then continued up the narrow trail to the ranch house, now well-worn with recent traffic.

"Remember, too, that his prediction was probably based on who you were, not who you are now."

Kyle smiled. "He knew me as the boy who couldn't sit still, who knew what he wanted to become, and always had his eye on the goal," he said. "That's still me, I guess, but my goal doesn't require me to go from assignment to assignment anymore. Having you in my arms is all the rush I need."

After parking beside the other vehicles, Kyle leaned over and kissed her. Just then, his brothers came out.

"Get a room!" Daniel yelled.

Kyle laughed. "Sorry. When the pressure's off, these guys can be real pains in the butt."

She chuckled. "Come on. You can introduce me to everyone."

For the first time, she met Preston's wife Abby, and Kendra, Paul's wife, as well as Gene and his wife, Lori. Holly was also there with Daniel.

Erin was soon hugged by everyone and welcomed into the family.

"I'm so glad things worked out the way they did," Holly whispered in her ear.

"Me, too," Erin answered with a happy smile.

While Kendra stayed outside watching the kids play, the others went back into the ranch house.

The men quickly gathered around Hosteen Silver's desk in anticipation.

"I pulled the letter meant for you out of the

drawer," Preston said, pointing to the envelope with Kyle's name on it.

"Are you sure you don't need someone to hold your hand?" Gene teased, and Daniel laughed.

Preston gave Kyle a pat on the back. "You might as well open it up, bro, cause it sure as hell isn't going away."

Kyle took the envelope and pulled out the note it contained. He read it silently first, then out loud.

"'Fox will journey to many places before Mother Earth calls him home to fulfill his destiny. Only then will he discover what has come to life at his feet and in his heart.'"

"As obscure as ever," Paul muttered.

"No, clear. It's about time you came home to stay, buddy," Daniel said. "The family business needs you."

"Or you could work at my ranch," Gene said.

"Me, a rancher?" Kyle laughed. "Sorry guy. I'm marrying a business manager slash chile farmer. That's as close to working with Mother Earth as I'll ever get."

"Maybe 'life at his feet' means Erin's chiles," Holly said.

"It may be more than that…" Erin said slowly. "Kyle helped me plant a desert rose outside. The pot had cracked, and replanting it here was the only option. Mind you, it has never been more

than one long stalk with some spindly leaves, s•
it may not have survived."

"Let's go see," Holly said.

Erin led the way outside, then hurried over and
crouched by the tiny plant. At the tip of its sol•
slender stalk was a small stem with new growth
and two leaves. In the center was a tiny perfectly
formed bud. "Look!"

"Even without that, I know my next move," Kyl•
said. Reaching into his pocket he brought out a
small box. "Erin, I love you," he said for only the
second time in his life. Then, getting down on one
knee, and offering her the box, added, "Will you
be my wife?"

She opened the box with trembling hands. Nes•
tled inside was a gold engagement ring with a tiny
heart-shaped diamond.

She drew in an excited breath. "Oh…"

"Is that a yes?" he asked.

"Yes!"

As he took her in his arms, his family encircled
them, patting him on the back and congratulat-
ing them.

"Kiss your bride-to-be, and come back inside
when you're ready," Holly said. "We'll celebrate!"

As soon as they were alone, Kyle smiled at her
"You already know I come with baggage—and a
big family. You sure you're ready for this?"

"It's exactly what I've always wanted," she whispered. "Now kiss me again."

He smiled and happily obliged. With her by his side, his world was complete. He'd traveled all over the globe, but what he'd needed most had been back home all along, waiting to be discovered.

* * * * *

LARGER-PRINT BOOKS!
GET 2 FREE LARGER-PRINT NOVELS PLUS
2 FREE GIFTS!

◆HARLEQUIN®

INTRIGUE®

BREATHTAKING ROMANTIC SUSPENSE

HILP13R

LARGER-PRINT BOOKS!

GET 2 FREE
LARGER-PRINT NOVELS
PLUS 2 FREE
MYSTERY GIFTS

Love Inspired®
SUSPENSE
RIVETING INSPIRATIONAL ROMANCE

Larger-print novels are now available...

YES! Please send me 2 FREE LARGER-PRINT Love Inspired® Suspense novels and my 2 FREE mystery gifts (gifts are worth about $10). After receiving them, if I don't wish to receive any more books, I can return the shipping statement marked "cancel." If I don't cancel, I will receive 4 brand-new novels every month and be billed just $5.24 per book in the U.S. or $5.74 per book in Canada. That's a savings of at least 23% off the cover price. It's quite a bargain! Shipping and handling is just 50¢ per book in the U.S. and 75¢ per book in Canada.* I understand that accepting the 2 free books and gifts places me under no obligation to buy anything. I can always return a shipment and cancel at any time. Even if I never buy another book, the two free books and gifts are mine to keep forever.

110/310 IDN F5CC

Name	(PLEASE PRINT)	
Address		Apt. #
City	State/Prov.	Zip/Postal Code

Signature (if under 18, a parent or guardian must sign)

Mail to the Harlequin® Reader Service:
IN U.S.A.: P.O. Box 1867, Buffalo, NY 14240-1867
IN CANADA: P.O. Box 609, Fort Erie, Ontario L2A 5X3

**Are you a current subscriber to Love Inspired Suspense books
and want to receive the larger-print edition?
Call 1-800-873-8635 or visit www.ReaderService.com.**

* Terms and prices subject to change without notice. Prices do not include applicable taxes. Sales tax applicable in N.Y. Canadian residents will be charged applicable taxes. Offer not valid in Quebec. This offer is limited to one order per household. Not valid for current subscribers to Love Inspired Suspense larger-print books. All orders subject to credit approval. Credit or debit balances in a customer's account(s) may be offset by any other outstanding balance owed by or to the customer. Please allow 4 to 6 weeks for delivery. Offer available while quantities last.

LISLPDIR13R

ReaderService.com

Manage your account online!

- Review your order history
- Manage your payments
- Update your address

> *We've designed
> the Harlequin® Reader Service
> website just for you.*

Enjoy all the features!

- Reader excerpts from any series
- Respond to mailings and
  special monthly offers
- Discover new series available to you
- Browse the Bonus Bucks catalog
- Share your feedback

Visit us at:
ReaderService.com